"Margo? Are you still there?"

"Yes." Barely.

"Catherine and I were hoping you'd come to the reception. We feel it's important for the children that they see this wedding has your support."

Did he know what he was asking? Margo rubbed her forehead. Forget the children being overwhelmed. What about her?

It was dizzying how fast her life had changed. She'd gone from being a married woman and practicing lawyer to a single mother with a business of her own. She'd adjusted—but was she ready to watch her ex-husband marry another woman?

And yet, she knew Tom had a point. For their kids' sake, she had to do this. "Give me the restaurant name and time and I'll be there."

Slipping the phone back into her apron, she leaned into her chair.

This was so unreal.

In the year they'd been living apart, Tom had had his affair with Janna, and now he was marrying someone named Catherine whom she had never met.

Her ex had been busy.

And in all that time, she hadn't gone on a single date.

Dear Reader,

When hearts break, dreams die and a marriage ends, sometimes the idea of loving again feels like an impossible fantasy. Especially when kids are in the picture.

Dating is challenging enough without adding the complication of children to the mix. Single parents are busy people. Working, raising kids and running a household all on your own leaves precious little time for dating. And yet, given the contemporary divorce rate this is the reality many of us face.

I'd like to welcome you to a new series about women (and men) who find themselves in this exact situation. In *Love and the Single Mom* you'll meet Margo Evans. Once Margo was full of hopes for her future. She studie law, became a lawyer, married a smart man and had two beautiful children. She thought she was living her dream—until her marriage fell apart.

Suddenly single, Margo reassesses her goals and decides to open a bistro. With two children and a new business to worry about, she definitely doesn't have time for dating. Or so she thinks…

I hope you enjoy this story, as well as the other books in SINGLES…WITH KIDS. If you would like to write or send e-mail, I would be delighted to hear from you through my Web site at www.cjcarmichael.com. Or send mail to the following Canadian address: #1754 - 246 Stewart Green, S.W., Calgary, Alberta, T3H 3C8, Canada.

Happy reading!

C.J. Carmichael

LOVE AND THE SINGLE MOM
C.J. Carmichael

HARLEQUIN®

TORONTO • NEW YORK • LONDON
AMSTERDAM • PARIS • SYDNEY • HAMBURG
STOCKHOLM • ATHENS • TOKYO • MILAN • MADRID
PRAGUE • WARSAW • BUDAPEST • AUCKLAND

ISBN-13: 978-0-373-71398-1
ISBN-10:   0-373-71398-3

LOVE AND THE SINGLE MOM

ABOUT THE AUTHOR

Hard to imagine a more glamorous life than being an accountant, isn't it? Still, C.J. Carmichael gave up the thrills of income tax forms and double entry bookkeeping when she sold her first book in 1998. She has now written over twenty novels for Harlequin Books and strongly suggests you look elsewhere for financial planning advice.

Books by C.J. Carmichael

HARLEQUIN SUPERROMANCE

SIGNATURE SELECT SAGA

*Return to Summer Island

To my good friends Ann and Dave Mallory.
Wishing you health, happiness and *bonne chance*.

CHAPTER ONE

Thursday's Soup of the Day:
Squashed Pear

THERE WAS THAT MAN AGAIN. As Margo Evans accepted change from a customer, her attention lingered on the guy who'd just entered her bistro. He was in his mid-thirties, dressed in a business suit. Just as he had yesterday, he claimed a table in the back near the kitchen even though several seats by the windows were available. Immediately he pulled out a newspaper and notepad from his briefcase, and before he'd even ordered anything to eat, his BlackBerry started to ring.

It was two-thirty in the afternoon. A slow time between lunch and rush hour. They had only one other customer, a woman in her forties who was reading a novel as she sipped her coffee. Still…the guy had his nerve.

Gritting her teeth, Margo pulled out the sign her daughter, Ellie, had made for her last night: No

Cell Phones Please. Ellie must have used every marker in the sixteen-color pack. It was a terrific sign. Margo taped it so that it hung down from the counter facing the guy in the suit.

But he was hunched over his BlackBerry and didn't notice.

How annoying. She didn't mind if her patrons took the occasional call, but if he planned to stay several hours, as he had yesterday, she was going to have to make him aware of the rules.

She went around the counter and slipped next to Emma Greenfield. Em's kids were in high school now and she worked Monday to Friday, eight hours a day. "Do we have a zucchini chocolate cake in reserve?"

"I think so."

"Good. Nora's stopping by for coffee later, and that's one of her favorites." Nora Clark was a new friend Margo had made a few months ago. One of the perks of owning a bistro was that she was always making new friends. But Nora was special. Like Margo, she was a single mom, too, and they always had lots to talk about.

"We've got the cake," Em assured her. "But we're running low on the soup."

Margo peered into the cauldron and saw that Em was right. They were down to the dregs, and if yesterday was anything to judge by, the guy in the suit was going to order several bowls of the stuff.

"Those soups of yours are the most popular item on the menu," Em said, as she wiped down the espresso machine. The beautiful red La Marzocco had been costly—even more than Margo's beloved Garland stove in the back—and Em treated it with the same attention that a car lover would bestow on a vintage automobile.

"Yes, the soup always sells out, doesn't it?" In fact, business was generally brisk and the feedback on the food was excellent. So why wasn't she making any money?

Margo couldn't figure it out. Lots of people had warned her about the work and the risks involved in starting a new business—particularly a restaurant, where hours were long and competition tight. Among those who had been the most cautious were the loans manager at the bank, her ex-husband Tom and her former associates at the law firm. She'd known they were right, but she hadn't appreciated just *how* right they would turn out to be.

Margo pulled the stainless steel soup container from its slot and headed for the kitchen. As she passed the guy in the suit, their eyes connected briefly.

Had they met before? Several times yesterday

she'd had the feeling that they had. For a moment it seemed as if he was going to say something to her, but then his BlackBerry beeped and he turned his attention back to that.

He looked like a typical businessman in his mid-thirties. The kind of customer she saw many times every day. He was conservative and clean-cut and totally boring....

Except for his eyes. His smile was kind of cute, too.

With her hip Margo pushed open the door to the narrow kitchen. Centered on the back wall was the stainless steel Garland. She stirred the pot of thick, fragrant squash and pear soup that simmered on the back burner, then refilled the cauldron and lugged it back to the serving area out front.

One of her regular customers was just walking in. Margo stopped to chat with the older gentle-man for a while and she smiled when he told her that his afternoon coffee was the highlight of his day.

"I always feel happy when I'm here," Oscar said in a whisper, as if it was something to feel ashamed of.

"So do I," Margo whispered back.

And she was. Her bistro was everything she'd ever dreamed it would be—except profitable. Margo had expected to lose money the first few months, but with a year of operation behind her she was getting desperate to creep out of the red.

The guy in the suit appeared at the counter as soon as she had the soup in place. He caught her eye. "Smells wonderful. I'll have a bowlful of that, plus another of those scones."

As she took his money, the recognition thing bugged her again. "Have we—?"

But before she could complete her question, his phone rang. He was wearing small earphones, so he was able to talk to whomever was on the line and carry his food back to his table all at the same time.

"That guy is starting to get on my nerves," Em commented quietly.

"Maybe I should take Ellie's sign and flash it in his face."

Em laughed. "Yeah. You do that."

"I'm serious." She started to lift the tape that was holding the sign to the counter, only to hear the sound of ringing yet again. It wasn't Suit Guy's BlackBerry this time—she was embarrassed to realize it was her own cell phone.

Em's hair was turning gray, but her eyebrows were still coal-black. She raised them now and Margo apologized.

"It might be an emergency. I'll just be a sec."

She withdrew to the kitchen where she pulled her phone from the pocket of her white apron. Only the kids' school and Tom had this number and they knew better than to use it casually.

Had one of the kids taken ill? Been injured on the playground? With a feeling of dread, Margo said hello.

"Margo?"

Not hearing the school secretary on the other end was a plus. But the familiar voice of her ex-husband didn't exactly fill her with joy. "Hi, Tom."

"Sorry to bother you at the bistro. But I needed to talk to you when the kids wouldn't be around."

Margo sank into a chair. This didn't sound like it was leading up to something good. "What's wrong?"

The final paperwork on the divorce had been signed last week. Everything had been running so smoothly lately that she hadn't expected to hear from Tom again in a long while.

"I've got some news. And I was wondering about the best way to tell Ellie and Peter."

This sounded big. Margo always wore her hair up at work, but she found a stray wisp and coiled it around her finger. "What is it?" Had he been transferred? Was he planning to move? Oh, God, give her strength if that was the case.

"I'm getting married."

"Wha—?" Margo's brain stalled. How could he be getting married? The ditzy paralegal he'd had his affair with had left their law firm in disgrace shortly after Margo's resignation. Ironically it was only Tom's career that had survived that scandal. "I didn't know you were still seeing Janna."

"I'm not. My fiancée's name is Catherine. She works part-time as a receptionist at Henry's firm."

Henry Kovatch was Tom's best friend. And supposedly one of hers, too. The three of them had been inseparable in law school. "Did Henry set you up?"

"Well…yes."

Hmm. Why hadn't Henry set *her* up with someone? Then again, the only people Henry knew were lawyers and people who worked with lawyers. And she definitely didn't want to get involved with another one of them.

"Catherine and I have been dating for about four months."

"That's all? And you want to get *married?*"

"I know it seems impulsive—"

"Seems?" Tom was the least impulsive person she'd ever known. On the other hand, he liked having a woman around to take care of him, which was one of the reasons their marriage had failed. Margo had expected to be an equal partner sort of wife. Not a mother fill-in. "This Catherine must be something else."

"She's wonderful. As soon as I met her I knew she was the one."

Margo closed her eyes. Tom had once said that about her. Did he remember?

He'd told her she was the prettiest, most amazing woman in the world and that nothing would make him happier than spending the rest of his life with her.

Apparently he'd meant his life or ten years, whichever came first.

Damn, she never had been one to read the fine print. Good thing she'd left the law. Like her marriage to Tom it was one of those things she'd thought she'd wanted, only to be disillusioned with the reality.

"Well…" *Spit it out, Margo.* "Congratulations. Have the kids met her?"

"Sure. They get along great."

Funny. Neither Ellie nor Peter had ever mentioned Catherine to *her.* Then again, neither had they mentioned anything about the new silver Audi roadster that Margo had seen in the garage the last time she'd dropped them off at Tom's for the weekend.

"Catherine loves them, too. This is going to

work out really well, Margo. I have no doubt about that."

God help them all if he was wrong. "So when is this wedding taking place?"

"That's the thing. See, we'd been planning a big church wedding, then last week we got the idea to do something simple and easy at city hall."

"Okay… But when?"

"That's what I needed to talk to you about. I know this is your weekend to have the kids, but I was hoping—"

"*This* weekend? You're getting married *this* weekend?"

"Would you calm down, Margo. Yes, I'm getting married this weekend. And I'd like the kids to be there."

In ten years of marriage, he'd never surprised her so much.

"If it's okay with you, I'll pick Ellie and Peter up after school on Friday—"

"That's *tomorrow.*" Did Ellie's pink dress shoes still fit her? Well, they'd have to. He'd left them no time to go shopping. "Do they know that you and Catherine are getting married?"

"Well, Catherine has practically been living with me the last few weeks, so I don't think they'll be too surprised."

"Tom—"

"Don't worry. I'm sure they'll be fine with it. Like I said, they *like* Catherine."

This was all so very *not* fine that Margo didn't have a clue where to start. The kids were going to be overwhelmed. A new stepmother, at the drop of a hat. How could Tom sound so cavalier about something that was going to totally change all of their lives?

Including hers.

Adjusting to a separate life from the father of her children was one thing. Having another woman in her children's lives was something else. Margo had known this would happen one day. She hadn't expected the day to arrive so soon, though.

"Margo? Are you still there?"

"Yes." Barely.

"Catherine and I were hoping you'd come to the reception, after city hall. We're having a few people to that new rooftop restaurant at Embarcadero Center and we feel it's important for the children that they see this wedding has your support."

Good God. Did he know what he was asking? Margo rubbed her forehead. Forget the children being overwhelmed. What about her?

It was dizzying how fast her life had changed this year. She'd gone from being a married woman and practicing lawyer, to a single mother with a business of her own. She'd adjusted marvelously—at least she felt she had—but was she ready to watch her ex-husband marry another woman?

And yet, she knew Tom had a point. For their kids' sake, she had to do this. "Give me the restaurant name and time and I'll be there."

Margo jotted down Tom's instructions, then wished him the best and disconnected the call. Slipping the phone back into her apron, she leaned into her chair and just sat.

This was so unreal.

In the year they'd been living apart, Tom had had his affair with Janna and now he was marrying someone named Catherine whom she had never met.

Her ex had been busy.

And in all that time, she hadn't gone on a single date.

CHAPTER TWO

Days Unemployed: 4

"DID YOU GET MY RÉSUMÉ? I faxed it to your office yesterday." As Robert Brookman spoke into his BlackBerry, he kept his eyes on the pretty blonde behind the counter.

He'd heard the older woman who served the coffee, and several of the other customers, refer to her as Margo. Which meant she must be the bistro owner.

Shifting his gaze to the notebook in front of him, he focused his attention back on his call.

"Great. Well, let me know as soon as you hear something." He said goodbye to his headhunter, then frowned. Finding a new job was going to take some time, he knew. He just wished Donald Macleod was a little more bullish about the job market in San Francisco right now.

He checked out the blonde again.

Margo. He liked the sound of the name. Just as

he liked the woman it belonged to. She greeted all her customers as if she was glad to see them. And he didn't think it was an act. She was just one of those naturally warm, sincere sort of people who enjoyed the company of others.

She was also a terrific cook.

He forced his gaze to the career section of the *San Francisco Chronicle.* He circled a few possibilities, then sent an e-mail to Donald. What Donald didn't understand was that Robert hadn't been unemployed since he'd graduated from college over ten years ago.

Though he'd lost his job through no fault of his own, and had received a nice compensation package in exchange, Robert didn't like the feeling of being out of work. He needed to get back behind a desk as soon as possible.

Robert finished his cup of coffee and considered requesting a refill. But at that moment, Margo disappeared into the kitchen. A moment later she reemerged, without her apron, and left the restaurant with a wave and a smile to the older woman behind the counter.

He checked the time. It was quarter past three. She'd left the bistro at this time yesterday, too. He sighed, then snapped shut his briefcase and pocketed the BlackBerry.

Tomorrow he'd just have to get here earlier.

It had been eight months since his breakup with Belinda and he was ready to move on. He'd tried dating a few women he'd met through work, but none of them had inspired much interest. Margo was the first to really capture his attention…and she didn't wear a wedding ring, so she seemed like a good candidate.

The only thing holding him back was the niggling feeling that he'd met her before. He wished he could recall where and when. Might save him some potential embarrassment when he finally worked up the nerve to ask her out.

USUALLY MARGO looked forward to seeing her children at the end of their day. Not today.

How unfair of Tom to leave the telling of his news to her. She was very afraid that the kids were going to be badly shocked. She could imagine Ellie stalking off in anger and Peter crying uncontrollably, the way he had when his father had first moved out of the family home.

Tell Daddy not to go.

He'd fallen to the floor with his sobs and Margo had picked him up. Hugged him and soothed him. Fortunately, with counseling, her children had recovered from that rough patch. But it was still a time Margo couldn't bear to think back on.

It was amazing to her that Tom was serious

about marrying someone she had never even heard the kids mention. Though, to be fair, the kids didn't talk much to her about what they did when they were at Tom's house. It was as if Ellie and Peter lived in two separate worlds, with no points of intersection between them.

Did other children of divorced parents act that way? Margo wished she had someone to ask. But the only single mom she knew—Nora—was widowed, not divorced.

Margo stopped on the corner next to the playground. Several other parents and caregivers were congregated here and she smiled at the father of one of her daughter's friends.

"Beautiful day, isn't it?"

"Can't beat spring time in San Francisco." Allan White was a stay-at-home dad. His wife happened to also be a lawyer. "Did Ellie get her book report done on time? Stephanie and I were up until eleven last night."

"Oh?" Ellie was such a responsible student that Margo rarely asked her about her homework. She was about to question Allan more about the project, when the school buzzer sounded. Soon kids were streaming out the doors, and Peter was one of the first.

A towhead like she had been at his age, he

wasn't as keen on his studies as his sister. He spotted her, grinned, then ran in her direction.

After a big hello hug, he asked if he could play while they waited for Ellie.

"Sure, honey." Margo watched as he raced toward the monkey bars, then swung his way toward his favorite slide. Ellie didn't show up for another ten minutes. As a fifth grade student, she felt she was too old to be walking home from school with her mother and baby brother. Privately Margo sympathized with her, but Tom was nervous about the South of Market neighborhood and so she continued to accompany the kids.

"Did you hand in your book report?" Margo asked her daughter when she finally showed up.

Ellie gave her a withering look that reminded Margo painfully of Tom. "Of course." Ellie took a brisk pace toward home, and Margo had to hustle Peter to follow her.

"Please slow down a little, Ellie. Your brother's legs aren't as long as yours."

Ellie said nothing to that, but she did reduce her speed marginally.

"So…" Margo still hadn't come up with a great way to tell them their father's news. Feeling awkward, she said, "I guess you guys know that your father has found someone that he really cares about."

Peter looked at her blankly.

"She means Catherine," Ellie explained over her shoulder.

"That's right. Catherine. Your father says you've had a chance to get to know her?"

Ellie shrugged. "Sort of."

"Well. Is she nice?"

"Sure," Peter said.

"She's okay."

"I'm glad you both like her."

Ellie stopped walking and eyed her suspiciously. "Why?"

Margo swallowed, but her mouth remained dry. "Your dad called me today and wanted me to tell you something."

Spit it out, Margo.

"Your father and Catherine have decided to get married." Margo swallowed again. "This weekend."

She waited for the fallout, but nothing happened.

"Cool," Ellie said, then resumed walking.

"Cool," Peter echoed, his eyes on his sister, as if he needed to gauge her reaction in order to determine his own.

"So you're okay with this?" Margo asked her daughter.

"Why wouldn't I be?"

Indeed. "Good."

That had been so much easier than she'd expected. And yet Margo didn't feel entirely satisfied with the children's reactions. Could it be she didn't *want* Catherine to be a nice person? That she would have been happier to have her children kick up a fuss?

Bitterness curdled on her tongue and she had the urge to lash out. To say something shallow and mean-spirited about Tom and the speed with which he'd replaced her. To disparage a woman she'd never even met.

Why…I'm jealous.

Margo was disappointed in herself, but she couldn't deny her own feelings. The truth was, she felt a little usurped by Catherine and she would have preferred it if her kids had said something even just a little negative about her.

Ellie and Peter were *hers*. She'd given birth to them and raised them and loved them. Just because Tom wanted another woman in his life didn't mean she and the kids did.

Only…maybe her kids *did* want Catherine in their lives. They hadn't given any sign that they didn't.

By the time they reached the bistro, Margo felt close to tears. She watched her kids scoot up onto stools where Em had milk and cookies waiting.

They attacked the snack like starving creatures. Lately it seemed Ellie couldn't get her hands on enough food, while her younger brother was always thirsty.

They were so cute. Peter with his missing front teeth and mischievous blue eyes. Ellie, so serious and grown-up acting, the way she'd always been, even as a baby.

Margo hated that their innocence was being marred by this divorce. Their father moving out had only been the beginning of the hurdles they would face, she now realized. Next would be the new stepmother. And possibly halfsiblings some-time down the road.

Feeling her anger toward Tom mounting, Margo made an excuse to go to the kitchen. The table at the back was now occupied by two young men in leather jackets and artfully disheveled hair. She wondered if she'd seen the last of Suit Guy and was surprised to realize she felt a bit disappointed at the idea.

In the kitchen she allowed herself to slam the copper pots around a little. Life was so unfair at times. She hated being divorced. Learning to share her time with the kids had been difficult enough. Now she had to stand on the sidelines as Tom moved on and married again.

The kitchen door swung open, and Em breezed

into the room. She pulled her apron over her head, then shoved it into the dirty laundry basket. "Sandy just showed up, so I'm off."

Margo knew "off" was a relative term. Em would be going home to prepare dinner for her husband and starving teenagers. Then she'd spend her evening either watching her son play basketball, or driving her daughter to dance lessons.

"We have some leftover muffins from the morning. Want to take them for the kids' lunches tomorrow?" Margo bagged them as she made the offer and Em accepted the package gratefully. A moment later Sandy—a college student with shoulder-length brown hair and serious, wide-set green eyes—popped in to grab an apron.

"It's quiet out there, thank goodness."

Margo could guess what she meant by that. "Edward hasn't shown up yet?"

"Second time this week." Sandy shook her head, slipped on the apron, then hurried back to the front.

Margo was glad she had Sandy to rely upon. Two months ago, Edward had seemed like a good hire. At first impression, he'd been good-natured, motivated and pleasant. But the day after she'd given him the job, he'd come to work with rings in his lip and eyebrow, as well as a stud through his tongue. Margo had nothing against self-expression, but it had seemed slightly deceitful to her that he had hidden his piercings for the job interview.

Lately, he'd been arriving late for work and shirking cleanup duties at the end of his shift. Today, when he finally arrived and came to the back to get an apron, he avoided eye contact with her.

"Hi, Edward. How are things?"

"Fine." He still didn't look at her.

"You've been running behind quite a bit lately. Is anything wrong?"

He shook his head, eyes still averted.

Margo sighed. "Are you sure there isn't a problem?"

"No. Everything's good."

Margo tilted her head to one side. If there was one thing she was sure about, it was this. Everything was *not* good. Not with Edward, not with the bistro and not with her life.

But how to begin tackling the problems, she had no idea.

A MESSAGE WAS WAITING for Robert on his machine when he got home from the gym. He dumped his sports bag near the closet, then hit the playback button, hoping the call would be from his headhunter. But the recorded voice was about thirty years too young for that.

"Hey, Robert, it's Andrew. Maybe you didn't get my other message, but I was wondering if you could come to my birthday party tomorrow? It's at six o'clock and Mom's making a chocolate cake. Well, she'll probably buy it, but it'll be chocolate for sure. Um…see you then. Bye."

Robert stared at the machine for several seconds, before erasing the message. Feeling like the biggest jerk on the planet, he hit the shower, trying not to remember Andrew's last birthday party.

He'd bought the boy a fishing pole and foolishly he'd made a bunch of promises, never dreaming that he might not be able to deliver on them. Even now he didn't know who'd been more excited about those pie-in-the-sky plans—him or Andrew.

Robert shut off the water, dried quickly then contemplated the remaining hours of the evening. He hadn't eaten, and after his workout, he was starving. There were some frozen entrées on hand, or he could call for take-out, but he found himself craving…soup.

The squashed pear soup at Margo's today had been delicious. Even better than the sunshine carrot from the day before.

As he made up his mind to go, Robert knew it wasn't just the food he was after. Sure it was good and the atmosphere at the bistro was warm and welcoming, but there was something more compelling pulling at him: the friendly woman who owned the place.

As he passed by the phone on his way out, he tried not to think of the boy who'd left him that message. He knew Andrew would be home, waiting and hoping, and his heart ached to think of that.

But what could he do? Belinda had said no contact, and she *was* the boy's mom.

FIFTEEN MINUTES LATER, Robert stepped inside Margo's Bistro. The place was small, holding ten tables, max, not counting the annex through an archway to his left. The colors of the decor were vivid, but the tones blended harmoniously—sort of like the flavors in Margo's soups.

Robert checked behind the counter. The older brunette he'd seen on his previous two visits wasn't on duty now. Instead, two college-aged kids were at work. The girl seemed to be hustling her buns off. The guy acted as if he was annoyed about something.

Robert scanned the rest of the room, disappointed when he didn't spot Margo. He'd taken a chance, hoping she might have returned for the evening, but it hadn't paid off.

Since he was here anyway, he lined up to place his order. Reflectively, he dug his hands into the pockets of his jeans. He touched a piece of cardboard and pulled out one of his old business cards.

Robert Brookman, MBA, Senior Account Manager, Wells Fargo.

Hard to believe that only last week this had been him. He'd been someone important, an employee at one of San Francisco's oldest and most prestigious banks. He'd been on his way up, a man bound for success.

He'd had an office and colleagues, a desk and a mound of work waiting for him at the start of every day. He'd taken pleasure in tackling and conquering those files before the closing of every night....

Robert Brookman, MBA, Senior Account Manager. That was who he was. Or who he had been. A busy, important person whose every minute of every day was spoken for.

Now he had the disorienting notion that if he suddenly disappeared, if someone walked into this bistro right now with a gun and forced him out into a waiting car, no one would notice. He could be gone a week, a month, hell even longer, and not a person would raise an alarm.

Robert scrunched the card, then pushed it back into his pocket.

"May I help you?" the pretty college student asked him.

"Yes, thanks." He ordered soup and a scone, then carried his food to the table at the back that he'd begun to think of as his. Two doors led off from the short hall at the rear of the restaurant. One was marked Employees Only. The other was the washroom. He sat with his back to both of them, then lifted a spoonful of the soup to his mouth.

It was good. Really, really good. He closed his eyes and savored the complex, complementary blend of flavors. Despite the amazing taste, though, he found he didn't have much of an appetite.

He set down his spoon and glanced through the arched opening. And that was when he spotted her.

Margo was sitting with another woman who also appeared to be in her mid-thirties—a woman with dark, reddish hair and a nice, slender body. She was very attractive, too, but Margo was the one who held his eye.

She was even prettier than he remembered. Curvier. Sexier.

But the dimples he'd noticed when she'd served him earlier that afternoon weren't much in evidence now. She and her friend seemed to be having a pretty intense conversation. He wondered what about.

He watched them surreptitiously for a while, and then he kicked himself. Two attractive women, about his age, sitting within a few yards of him? What was he waiting for?

Robert slid his chair back and got to his feet.

CHAPTER THREE

"Phew. Sorry about that." Margo sank into the rattan couch next to Nora after running upstairs to check on the kids. On the table in front of them was the chocolate zucchini cake and a packet of photographs she'd put there earlier.

"No problem," Nora assured her. "Everything okay?"

"Both sound asleep." Stairs from the bistro kitchen ran up to the door of their apartment so it was easy for Margo to run back and forth. It was like being on different levels in a multi-level home, but just to be cautious Margo also had a two-way monitor set up so they could talk to one another if needed. She placed the small receiver on the table, next to the cake. "So how was your week?"

"Busy." Nora sighed. "Like usual."

As well as being the mother of an active little boy, Nora had a full-time job as a physiotherapist. On top of all that, her sister was living with her but not paying her share of the household expenses.

"How are Suzanne's wedding plans coming along?"

"I'm not sure. Suzanne's being a little cagey lately. I hope her fiancé knows what he's getting into. I love my sister, but—"

She didn't need to say any more. Suzanne was a charming person, but not exactly reliable where money was concerned.

"So how about you, Margo?" Nora helped herself to a piece of the cake, then lost no time digging in to it.

"It's been one of those days…."

"Oh?"

"I had a call from my ex. But first, take a look at these." Margo slipped the photographs from their packet. "I had the pictures from last week's party developed. There are some really cute ones of Danny."

Like any proud mother, Nora reached for the pictures eagerly. She'd oohed and aahed through about half of them when she suddenly stopped. Leaning close to Margo she whispered, "Who is that guy? In the back. The one staring at you?"

Margo felt a prickling at the base of her neck. Not a creepy, icky prickling, but a sensual, exciting sort of *tingle*.

She knew without looking.

He'd come back.

She pretended to check out the washroom door. Yes, it was Suit Guy, only he wasn't dressed in his suit now, but in jeans and a T-shirt and he looked *hot.*

Suddenly she became very aware of the ambiance in the room. In the daytime, when sunlight streamed in from the floor-to-ceiling windows and highlighted the lemon tree and the hibiscus, the bistro's annex room had the feel of a greenhouse.

At night, however, when she drew the ginger-colored curtains and lit the candles, then the annex was transformed into an intimate, slightly exotic place—a world away from the bustle of cosmopolitan San Francisco on the other side of the walls.

In short, it became a room perfect for romance....

"Is he looking this way?" she asked Nora.

"Not anymore. Now he's eating his soup. Do you know him?"

"He came in yesterday, then again this afternoon. But the answer is no. I don't know him." That shadow of a memory just would not take substantial shape. She wondered if perhaps she just *wished* she'd met him before.

"Would you like another piece of cake?" Margo asked. Nora was already finished her first and was sipping on her chai latte.

"Forget the cake. How long has it been since you've been on a date?"

"Are you *trying* to be cruel?" No one knew better than Nora the pathetic state of her social life. That was one of the subjects they often talked about—how hard it was to meet men when you had kids and worked full-time.

Sometimes Margo wondered if that part of her life was over for good.

"Wait." Nora tried to appear blasé. "He's looking this way again."

"Probably at *you*."

"No way. This one is yours, Margo. What are you going to do about it? He's coming this way."

"He is not." But he *was*. Margo couldn't believe it. She set down her fork, but in her nervousness, she knocked aside the photographs she and Nora had been looking at.

Several of the glossy four-by-sixes fell to the floor.

Suit Guy scooped them up as if he'd crossed the room for exactly that purpose. Before handing them over, he glanced at the photos and frowned.

"Thank you." Margo accepted the pictures and set them on the table. "That was clumsy of me."

The guy had boy-next-door looks, except for his eyes, which were darkly lashed and deeply blue. Right now those eyes seemed to be looking at everything in the room except her.

"No problem. I was just coming by to, uh, to tell you how much I enjoy your soups. Do you make them here?"

Soup? He'd crossed the room to ask about soup? Margo shot an "I told you this wasn't what you thought it was" look at Nora. "Sure. We have a different special every day, and they're all my own recipes. I'm glad you like them."

"The best I've ever tasted."

She sensed Nora grinning at her and her face grew hot. "By the way, I'm Margo."

"Yeah. I assumed as much. From the name of the place."

Margo felt her face grow hotter. "Margo *Evans*," she clarified.

"Robert Brookman," he said before shaking first her hand, then Nora's.

Realizing she hadn't introduced her friend, Margo added quickly, "And this is my friend, Nora Clark."

Robert asked Nora a few questions and seemed keenly interested. Margo sank back into the cushions of the sofa and prayed desperately for Sandy or Edward to call her with an emergency from the kitchen. She'd *known* Robert wasn't looking at *her*. He liked her soups. Not her.

When Robert found out Nora was a physiotherapist, he told her about a buddy with a sore knee. Nora gave him the name of a colleague who ought to be able to help, then scribbled a number on the back of one of her business cards.

"Thanks a lot." Robert pocketed the card. "Well, I should be going. Sorry to interrupt, but it was good to meet you, Nora. You, too, Margo."

He left without giving either of them a backward glance.

ROBERT HIT THE SIDEWALK and kept on walking. He didn't care where he went, he just needed to move. That had been close. Damn close. He'd gone to that table intending to ask Margo out, but one look at those pictures had changed his mind.

What if those were her kids?

He couldn't get involved with another single mom. Hell, what if she was married? He hadn't even thought of that. They ought to make the wearing of wedding bands a legal requirement. It sure would make the life of a single man a heck of a lot easier.

After a while, when he'd blown off the worst of the adrenaline rush, Robert slowed his pace. He noticed a boutique cycle shop ahead and went to gaze in the window.

A sweet little two-wheeler, a BMX just like

Andrew wanted, was in the display window. Maybe he could buy it for his birthday. Belinda had said no contact—but he could have it delivered....

Imagining the delight Andrew would feel getting that bike, Robert was sorely tempted.

But no. He might not be breaking the letter of Belinda's request, but he would definitely be breaking the spirit.

Reluctantly Robert turned away from the window. He checked out the street signs at the next intersection, got his bearings, then headed toward home. He walked slowly, in no rush to get there.

Oddly enough, he found himself thinking of Margo again. Damn, why hadn't he just asked her? *Are you married? Are these your kids?* He'd been caught so off balance, all he'd managed to do was chat up the physiotherapist. And he wasn't even interested in her.

Well, he'd be better off forgetting about both of them, he decided. He'd really blown things tonight.

AFTER ROBERT LEFT the bistro, Margo turned a blank face to Nora. "Was it something I said?"

Nora laughed. "Actually, I think it was something he *saw*." She tapped the photographs. "He definitely got cold feet after he picked up these."

"I don't know how cold his feet were. He left with your phone number."

"That was just business. I get that reaction all the time when people find out what I do for a living."

Margo wasn't so sure.

"Trust me," Nora added. "He was planning to talk to you until he saw those pictures. Maybe he's worried you're married."

Maybe. Margo looked at her ringless hands. Somehow she didn't think that was it. "Oh, well. He looked kind of dull, don't you think?"

"Not really."

"You should have seen him in his suit." In his dark blue pinstripe, Robert Brookman had appeared to be of the same ilk as her ex—a business-obsessed workaholic who scheduled evenings out with his wife with less frequency than his semi-annual dental checkups.

"I bet he looked really hot in his suit, too."

Margo wouldn't admit that Nora was right. "It's probably just as well. My life is too hectic for romance, anyway. If he calls you, make sure you say yes."

"I keep telling you—it's not me he's interested in. But even if he was…I'm not sure I'm ready to start dating yet."

Nora's expression grew sad and Margo knew she was thinking about Kevin.

Nora didn't talk about him much. All Margo knew was that he'd been a cop, killed in a car accident before Danny's birth. It was a loss from which Nora didn't seem fully recovered. But Margo hoped that she would move on soon.

Kids were terrific. A job you loved was great, too. But there were times when Margo longed for more and she knew Nora did, too. With a sigh, she picked up her fork and took another taste of cake.

After a moment's silence, Nora said, "Weren't you going to tell me something about your ex?"

Good lord. How could she have forgotten? "I need more coffee before I get into that story. Hang on a minute."

Margo hurried to the other room and slipped behind the counter. No customers were waiting in line at the moment so she had free access to the espresso machine. Sandy was clearing tables, while Edward made a show of rearranging the goodies in the display case.

A few minutes later Margo returned to the annex room with a fresh chai latte for Nora and a top-up to her mocha.

"So…?" Nora prodded.

"You'll never believe this." Margo settled back

into the couch, then took a deep breath. "Tom's getting married again."

Nora looked shocked. "But didn't you say his affair with the bimbo was over?"

"Apparently he started dating someone else, about four minutes after the first affair ended. The new bimbo is named Catherine and she works part-time in reception at a law firm. That's all I know about her."

Nora leaned closer as Margo relayed her conversation with Tom, practically word for word. "I'm just stunned," she concluded. "I can't believe my children are going to have another mother."

"No—no, don't say that," Nora insisted. "*You're* their mother. Not this Catherine person."

"But what about when the kids spend time with their father?" Margo set the mocha down. Even chocolate, coffee and whipped cream couldn't entice her tonight. "You don't know Tom. He's a traditional guy. He'll expect Catherine to do all the cooking and cleaning up. She'll be the one making Ellie's and Peter's lunches for school and washing their laundry and oh…"

Margo made a weird noise—she wasn't sure if it was a sob or a choked laugh. "Listen to me, complaining about another woman doing the chores that I get so tired of sometimes. But as much as I hate the weekly grind of laundry and lunches, I hate even more the idea of Tom's new wife doing it."

Nora squeezed her hand. "I understand."

"Do you?" Margo was still grappling with the enormity of this thing. "From now on my kids will be going on vacations with this woman. They'll see new places with her, share new experiences. All without me."

"But you'll go on vacations with them, too."

"That isn't the point. The kids are little and I'm their mom. I don't want to miss the first time they go skiing. Or visit a dude ranch. Or see Washington D.C."

These were all trips she and Tom had at one time planned to take with their children. Now he'd be doing all that with Catherine.

"Poor Margo, I don't know what to say. I'd go crazy in that situation," Nora admitted.

Margo knew that she would. Although it was awful that Nora's husband was dead, at least she didn't have to worry about joint custody arrangements or stepparents or any of that messy stuff.

"Does Catherine have children?"

Good question. "I don't think so."

"Hopefully your kids won't have stepsiblings to worry about." Nora was working hard to find something positive to say.

"But that means Catherine will be clueless about kids."

"True. Like in that movie *Stepmom,* when Julia Roberts's character is so insensitive in the beginning."

"Not to mention the real mother *dies* in that movie," Margo pointed out.

"Okay, so that was a bad example. Sorry. I really am trying to make you feel better. Eat some more cake. I'm sure this Catherine will turn out to be a very nice woman."

Margo took a bite of cake and wondered why neither Nora's comforting words nor chocolate seemed to help.

"You need a distraction. Like that guy, Robert Brookman…"

"The guy who couldn't get out of here fast enough once he saw a picture of my children?"

"Maybe I was wrong about that. As you said, he was probably worried that you might be married and just choosing not to wear a ring."

"That's an optimistic interpretation."

"Tell you what," Nora said. "If he comes by again tomorrow, you'll know he's interested. If he doesn't…then start looking for someone else."

"Someone else? I thought we'd just established the fact that neither of us have time for a man in our lives right now?"

"Hey, you were the one complaining about your ex-husband's new fiancée. Don't you know that the best defense is a good offence? Instead of worrying about the new woman in Tom's life, I say you make him worry about the new man in yours."

CHAPTER FOUR

Friday's Soup of the Day: Sherry Chanterelle

ROBERT STOPPED TO READ the specials in the bistro window. He'd always loved mushroom soup, he told himself as he went inside.

He couldn't say what he was doing back here. The soup was a convenient excuse, but he knew better. He paused at the sight of Margo serving an older man. The two bantered with a degree of familiarity that made him unaccountably envious.

He wanted her to smile like that at him.

No question about it, he had it bad. Wouldn't he feel like a fool, though, when he found out she was married with a parcel of kids? He joined the queue waiting to be served and plotted the best way to find out what he'd come here to learn.

HE WAS BACK. Margo saw him on the street as he stopped to read the specials on the chalkboard. When he stepped inside, her heart felt like it was dancing. Nora had been right after all…or had she?

Robert's smile when he stepped up to the counter seemed guarded.

"Hi, Margo. Could I have a bowl of the soup and a scone on the side?"

She took his money while Em filled the order. She glanced up once at Robert, but he wasn't even looking in her direction. Maybe he really was here for the soup.

Robert carried his tray to the table at the back and, like before, he set himself up with the daily paper and his BlackBerry. She tried to ignore him after that, but it wasn't easy. As before, he stayed for a long time. Once or twice she thought she saw him looking her way, but she couldn't be sure.

After the lunch hour rush was over, Margo decided to go back to the kitchen to experiment with a new muffin recipe. She envisioned a combination of dried cherries, dark chocolate and pecans swirled into a batter of wholesome grains and buttermilk.

The challenge of concocting something new was just what she needed to take her mind off Robert Brookman. Not to mention Tom's upcoming wedding.

As she scooped chunks of dark chocolate into the batter, Margo glanced out the open door at

Robert's back. She wondered how much longer he would stay. And what was he working on so intently? She couldn't complain about him taking up a table since he continued to order food. So far he'd had two bowls of soup, three scones and four cups of coffee.

He'd also covered his table with newspapers and his laptop, and had taken half a dozen different phone calls. It was almost as if he'd decided to make her bistro his new office. And, cute as he may be, she wasn't too happy about that.

Gently, Margo stirred the chocolate, cherries and nuts through the batter. It was thicker than most muffin batters, but if she added extra liquid now, she'd end up overmixing and ruining the muffins anyway. She'd just have to hope for the best.

Margo scooped the mixture into muffin liners, then put the tray in the oven. As she set the timer for twenty minutes, she noticed that it was almost three-thirty. Tom and Catherine would be picking the children up from school soon. Hopefully everything would go smoothly, but she couldn't help worrying about Peter and Ellie.

Yesterday they'd acted as if their dad's remarriage was no big deal, but the reality would surely hit soon. This could be terribly confusing for them.

As she ran a sink of soapy, hot water for the

dirty dishes, Margo wondered if the family was due for another round of counseling. Maybe she'd discuss the idea with Tom when he and Catherine came back from their honeymoon.

Honeymoon...

They'd probably go someplace with five stars and 600-count bedsheets—a total contrast from her and Tom's camping expedition in Marin County. They'd been college students with not much time between semesters, and even less money. They'd hiked in the mornings and spent their afternoons sleeping on the beaches and making love whenever they wanted. She'd been so happy and so optimistic about the future. But whoever dreamed on their honeymoon that divorce lay in the future?

"Something smells good in here."

She whirled around to find Robert Brookman in her kitchen, just an arm's length away. He looked different in the small galley space. Even better than she remembered.

Maybe it was *me he was interested in...* "Can I help you?"

"I hope so. I was just—"

The loud buzz of the timer startled them both. Margo rushed to switch it off. "Sorry. I'm experimenting with a new recipe."

She pulled the tray from the oven and her earlier

fears were confirmed. The muffins were too flat. Even without checking, she could tell the consistency was going to be tough.

Robert inspected them, too. "They look smaller than the ones in your front display case."

"I know. Something definitely went wrong." She dumped the muffins out onto a clean cloth, wrote a few quick comments in her notebook then looked up at Robert. "Feeling brave? Want a taste?"

"I'm your man."

The double entendre hit them at the same moment. Their glances collided, then they both looked quickly away.

"Actually," Robert said, clearing his throat, "I realized something a few minutes ago. Ever since I saw you I've been trying to think why you look so familiar. About a year ago you had a line of credit approved at the Wells Fargo branch down the block from here, didn't you?"

Margo froze. Great. This was exactly the link from the past that she did not need right now. Robert Brookman was from Wells Fargo. But now that he'd mentioned that, she remembered, too. She nodded reluctantly.

"I was on a branch tour. When I'd stopped to talk with your loan officer, I hadn't realized he was busy with a customer."

Busy with *her*. She recalled Robert apologizing for interrupting, then asking the loan manager to come talk to him when he had a few minutes. Ten seconds Robert had been in that office. Fifteen, tops. And yet, he'd remembered her.

"I checked over your file that day. I remember being surprised that a lawyer would decide to abandon her law career and open a restaurant."

"You're not the only one who was surprised by that decision. Most of my friends and family felt I was taking a terrible risk."

Robert glanced out the open door to the room full of customers. "Your gamble seems to have paid off."

She dropped her gaze for a moment. If only he knew the truth. "We're pretty busy."

"I'm not surprised. Your food is terrific. Especially the soup. But I've already told you that."

"Thank you." She wondered if that was what he was doing here. Checking up on her business on behalf of the bank. "I haven't missed any of my loan payments."

"Relax. I'm not here in an official capacity." He tugged on his tie, and suddenly he was the one who looked uncomfortable. "Actually, I don't work for the bank anymore. I was laid off last Friday."

He tried to look as if this wasn't any big deal,

but Margo could tell it was. "I'm sorry to hear that."

"Yeah, well, the company was downsizing and I happened to be a recent hire since I just moved from Seattle a year ago."

"What brought you to San Francisco?"

"A woman—my old girlfriend." He shrugged. "She isn't in the picture anymore, by the way."

He gave her a questioning look then, and Margo knew he was wondering about her. Suddenly nervous, she switched the subject. "Would you like something to drink? Water or juice?"

"Water would be fine."

She filled two glasses, then invited him to sit at the stainless steel counter with her. "I've been wondering what you've been working on every day, with your newspapers and laptop and all those calls."

"I'm looking for a new job."

She connected the final dot. "And you're using my bistro as your job search headquarters." Here was her chance to voice her objections, but all of a sudden she found she didn't have any.

"Well, the coffee's good and the food's even better. Then there's the atmosphere…"

He was looking at her in a very intense way. As if it wasn't just the place he liked…but her. Margo gripped the edge of the steel counter, welcoming the feel of the solid, cold metal.

She ought to be encouraging him. A little flirting wouldn't hurt. Instead she found herself panicking. Maybe she wasn't ready to start dating, after all. "I don't suppose you've noticed the sign I have hanging on my counter out front. The one that says, "No cell phones please." My daughter made it."

"Your daughter."

That seemed to bring him up cold.

"So the kids in the pictures last night are yours?"

"Two of them are. My son Peter is seven and Ellie is ten."

His gaze dropped to her hands.

She swallowed, then added, "I'm divorced. It's been about a year. My ex and I have joint custody of our children."

"Oh." He tugged on his tie again. "I'm never sure what to say to that. Sorry or congratulations." He smiled nervously.

"To tell you the truth, I'm not sure, either." According to the statistics, half of all marriages ended in divorce. But she'd never imagined that hers would be one of them.

She needed to change the subject. "So…how's the job search going?"

He looked glad that she'd asked. "I've got a headhunter working for me and I've been calling a bunch of people I know, too. But so far I haven't managed to nab so much as a first interview. They tell me the job market is tight right now. At least in banking."

"I'm sure you'll find something soon."

He sighed. "I hope so. I graduated in the top ten percent of my class. Always got great performance reviews at both of the banks where I've worked in the past."

"It hasn't even been a week," she reminded him gently. "Maybe this is an opportunity for you to take a little breather. Reassess your goals and your plans for the future."

"Well, I did go sailing on Tuesday."

"You took off a whole day, huh?"

He smiled at her teasing. "I made a few calls from the marina. So the day wasn't a total waste. But seriously, I don't need to think about my plans. I know what I want. No doubt about that."

The confidence in his voice was compelling, but as Margo met his gaze, she was struck again with the incongruous notion that he was talking about *her,* and not the job at all.

She swallowed. "You know—"

They were interrupted again, this time by the ringing of the bistro's phone. She went to answer it and was dismayed to find herself talking to a credit manager from Wells Fargo. As she conducted the brief conversation, Robert took a bite from one of the muffins. He didn't look impressed. She turned her back to him.

"Three weeks. Yes, I understand. Goodbye." She stared at the phone on the wall for a few moments. In her mind she pictured the account book upstairs, the files of loan statements and growing pile of unpaid bills.

"Bad news?"

Pride almost made her fib. But what was the point? Robert was a banker, maybe he could give her a few pointers. "You know how I said that I was making my loan payments?"

His expression grew serious. "Yes?"

"Well, I have been. But not the full amount. I was hoping to renegotiate my monthly payments. But now the bank wants to see my cash flow projections for the upcoming year. And they want them in three weeks."

"Let me guess. You don't have cash flow projections."

"Should I?" He didn't need to answer. She could see by his expression that she should. "Oh, Lord. I can barely keep up with the bills, the tax remittances and monthly payroll."

"Are you doing all that yourself?"

"Partially. I bought a computer package that was supposed to integrate everything…accounting, payroll, taxes, inventory… But I'm not using it to its potential."

"Restaurants survive or fail based on certain key numbers. Inventory management is one. Meal costing is another."

"Yes, I know. I've read the manual that came with the package." Well, she'd *skimmed* the manual. She simply didn't have the time to go through it in detail. "Once I've got my feet on the ground, I'm going to hire an accountant."

Robert gave her an incredulous look. He glanced up, as if inspecting the ceiling, then down to the concrete floor. Finally, he said, "I realize we haven't known each other very long. But there's something I have to tell you."

Margo guessed this wasn't going to be good news. "Yes?"

"You can't wait until you have money saved in the bank. You need to hire an accountant now, or you'll *never* get your feet on the ground."

Margo knew Robert's suggestion was well-intended. But he just didn't have a clue. "I don't have the money for any extra expenses."

Robert considered that. "How about free soup and scones? Maybe the occasional cup of coffee, too."

Was he offering to help her? "But you're a banker, not an accountant."

"Close enough. I've seen tons of cash flow statements. I ought to be able to figure out how to prepare one."

She was sure he could. Better and faster than she could, anyway. "But—"

"It's not as if I'm particularly busy right now," he pointed out. "This'll help fill my time until I get a real job."

"That's a generous offer. But it wouldn't be fair for me to accept." It might not be fair. But it was tempting. She'd love to put all the accounting worries behind her and focus on the jobs she knew how to do well.

"Are you worried about taking advantage of me?"

His eyes sparkled with humor and she knew she wasn't imagining the double meaning this time. "You should be so lucky, Robert Brookman."

He gave her a once-over. A thorough study that began with her swept-up hair and ended with the polished pink toes peeking out from her espadrilles.

"Yeah, you're right. I should be so lucky. In the meantime, why don't you show me your books and let me see if I can help?"

"Well...if you're sure." She led the way upstairs

to the apartment she shared with the kids. It was a three-bedroom and quite roomy, but there was no space for a separate office, so she'd set the computer up in a corner of the living room.

The raspberry-colored sofa faced the television. On the opposite wall, a dark-blue, stained wooden armoire held the computer. Next to that was an open-shelf unit filled with labeled baskets. "Here's where I keep my records."

Robert pulled one of the baskets off the shelf. It was crammed full of unpaid invoices. He looked at her and raised his eyebrows.

"I'm just a little behind on those." She brushed past him to open the doors of the armoire and power up the computer. Above the computer was a shelf where she kept important reference books.

"Here's the manual," she said brightly. "One good thing about not having much room… everything's at your fingertips."

He put his hand on the book, which happened to bring his hand right next to her breast. She caught her breath, felt a zap of pure, physical reaction. Looking up, she saw his gaze on the scooped neck of her top.

Speaking of things being right at someone's fingertips…. The double entendres were killing her today.

She thrust the book at him, then backed away. "You wanted to dive right in...well, here you go." She headed for the stairs. "I'll be right back with some coffee."

CHAPTER FIVE

ROBERT FELT LIKE banging his head on the desk the moment Margo left the room. What was he doing here? Margo might be divorced, but she had two kids. This woman was off-limits.

Why had he offered to help her?

He leaned back in the chair and looked around the place. Pictures of Margo's children were everywhere, reminding him of the folly of what he was doing. After his experience with Belinda and Andrew, how could he be getting involved with another single mother?

Robert studied the pictures on the wall. Unlike studio-variety photographs, these were candid shots, taken from unusual angles, each of them capturing something unique and special. In one, Margo's daughter hung upside down from a monkey bar. In another, a shot had been taken from above, Margo's son as a baby, playing with bubbles in his bath.

Robert took a deep breath.

He didn't have to stay. She wasn't paying him anything. He could find another coffee shop to hang out in until he was back working again.

But there was something about Margo that had drawn him in and it wasn't just the enticing aroma of her homemade soups.

His gaze fell on a photograph of her with her children. They were sitting on a wooden porch step. She had her arms around them in a protective, motherly pose. Her head was angled to the camera and her blond curls covered one of her fabulous blue eyes. Her smile seemed so real, it made him feel warm inside just to look at it.

He enjoyed looking at her. Talking to her. Just being around her. And she seemed to like him, too—if he discounted that one comment about cell phones.

If only she didn't have kids….

He'd never even considered the danger when he'd been dating Belinda. Andrew's father never bothered to see him, so with hindsight it was easy to understand why the boy had taken to Robert so quickly. Ignorant of the potential danger, Robert had welcomed this first instance of hero worship. In fact, he'd reveled in it.

He'd always planned on having children, but before Andrew, his desire to do so had been theoretical in nature. Andrew had given him a real-life taste of the pleasures of fatherhood. Robert could still remember the first time Andrew had fallen asleep in his arms. The three of them had been watching a movie on the living room sofa. Andrew had turned from the television with a yawn, and the next thing Robert knew, the little boy's head was nestled against his chest.

His heart couldn't have been filled with more love if that child had been his own flesh and blood.

He brushed a hand over his face and gave himself a mental kick. The truth was, since their breakup, he missed Andrew a hell of a lot more than Belinda.

If it was up to him, he would have continued spending time with Andrew. But Belinda wanted her son to bond with the new man in her life. And she felt that would never happen if he continued to visit Robert.

Maybe she was right. Maybe not. But she was Andrew's mother and this was her call to make. What was in Robert's control was the power to avoid situations like this in the future.

So…he should leave.

But he couldn't. He sensed Margo was in a real jam here. And he had the time to help her. He pulled out one of the wicker baskets and riffled through it. Seemed like an awful lot of unpaid bills. He tried a different basket. These invoices had been paid, but hadn't been entered into the computer. He checked through the stack and saw that she was several months behind with the record keeping. Better start with the bank statements....

He looked for those, then became so engrossed in the work, that he barely heard the squeak of the stairs, or the sound of footsteps moving toward him.

"I brought you a brownie with your coffee."

Margo spoke in hushed tones as if afraid to interrupt his train of thought. Though he didn't look up, he could smell the citrusy scent of her perfume and he felt the brush of her arm against his as she set the coffee cup and plate on the desk.

Immediately, he lost all track of what he was doing. Before he could say anything to her, though, she was gone, hurrying down the stairs back to her customers.

He stared at the paper in his hand, and when it continued to remain meaningless, set it down. He took a bite of the brownie, then a swallow of coffee.

Children, he reminded himself. Margo has two children. You can't get involved with her.

He raised his gaze to a picture of Ellie and Peter with their arms around a huge tree trunk. The tree was too thick for their hands to meet. Both kids were laughing.

Based on all these photographs they seemed like happy, well-adjusted kids. Why wouldn't they be, with a mother like Margo?

Belinda had been a good mother, too, but she'd emphasized rules and order just a little too much, he'd thought. Margo definitely didn't seem like that. He guessed she would be fun and exciting and…passionate.

Robert groaned. Even if he took a chance on Margo and things worked out, blended families were always complicated. And if things didn't work out, the kids were bound to end up getting hurt.

Concentrate on the business and forget about the woman. He did his best to follow his own advice for the next few hours. In fact, he was so preoccupied that the next time Margo came up, he was surprised to discover it was six-thirty.

"How can you work in the dark like that?" Margo switched on a lamp by the desk. She swept her hair off her forehead and sank into one of the easy chairs. She looked exhausted.

But also sexy and appealing….

He saved his work on the computer, then swiveled his chair to face her. "Long day?"

"Very. And one of my employees on the

evening shift showed up late again." She worried her bottom lip. "I hope I'm not going to have to fire him."

"Why not? You can always hire someone else."

"I wish it was that easy. I'm discovering that good employees are very difficult to find." She eyed the computer. "Well, how bad was it? I'm surprised you didn't run out of here screaming hours ago."

"I'm still entering data into the computer. You know, if you did this every month, it wouldn't be such an enormous job. Come here, and I'll show you."

Margo moved closer and he wondered if this was such a good idea. He definitely thought straighter when there were a few feet between them. Quickly he took her through the steps she should be following every month. She caught on quickly.

"I try to set aside a little time for record keeping every night," she admitted. "But when you have kids, it's not so easy. By the time they're ready for bed, I am, too."

She sighed, then pushed herself out of her chair. "How does a glass of wine and some herbed goat cheese sound?"

Robert swallowed as she pulled off her apron to reveal her curvy figure. He had to get out of here before he clouded his intentions with a glass of that wine.

But before he'd risen from his chair, Margo was in the kitchen, decanting a bottle. Deftly she poured some into two glasses, then handed him one.

They clicked glasses together, then drank. He could feel the blood pounding in his ears. He knew he had to leave, but his feet were rooted like tree stumps.

Margo returned to the kitchen, where she prepared a plate of cheese and crackers. She came back to the sofa and he found himself sitting next to her. They chatted about the weather, baseball and movies.

Then she glanced at her watch and he saw her jaw tighten.

"What's wrong?"

She hesitated. "My kids are at their dad's tonight, getting ready for a wedding ceremony tomorrow. I was just wondering how they're handling everything."

He took another swallow of the wine. *Get out of here, Robert,* his wiser half cautioned. He ignored the warning. "Your ex is getting remarried?"

"Yeah."

"That must feel weird."

She laughed. "Yeah."

Crazy guy, Robert found himself thinking, as he watched Margo tip her head back and enjoy another mouthful of the light Chablis. Why would any guy married to Margo let her go? She was pretty, sexy and a damn good cook.

And even when she was in a funk—as she obviously was right now—she was still good-humored about it.

He watched as Margo spread creamy cheese over thick crackers. She slipped from the sofa to the floor, stretched out her legs and leaned back her head. He stared at the golden curls that spilled oh-so-close to the hand he had resting on one of the seat cushions. After a moment, he sat on the floor next to her.

"Her name is *Catherine,*" Margo said, making it sound like a confession. "The kids seem to like her, but I don't know."

"You're not so keen on her?"

"We haven't even met."

"Does that worry you?"

"A little. What if she turns out to be awful? You hear such horror stories about stepmothers."

"Yeah, I know. But most stepfamilies get sorted out eventually, don't they? My mom raised me on her own, but a lot of my friends' parents were divorced. Most of them did just fine…despite the statistics that seem to indicate otherwise."

"Oh, God, I hope you're right." Margo topped up their wineglasses. "Even though Tom and I have been apart for a year, sometimes I still can't believe my life ended up this way. Tom and I were supposed to be *forever.* And now he's getting married to someone else." She forced a laugh. "And he wants me to go to the reception after."

"Really?" Robert tried to imagine attending Belinda's wedding to the new guy who'd replaced him. "That doesn't sound like fun."

"Especially since I don't have a—"

She didn't finish. But her eyes met his and he knew what she had been planning to say. She didn't have a date to take to her ex-husband's wedding reception.

Well, that was too bad for her, but it had nothing to do with him.

Except, he felt badly on her behalf and he didn't know why. Just as he couldn't really explain why he'd offered to do her cash flow statements for her.

He tried not to notice her cleavage as she reached for a cheese-smeared cracker. Her hair was a mess, and she seemed to realize it at just that moment, because she released the clip at the back of her head and blond curls tumbled to her shoulders.

Oh, God. He really shouldn't do this.

"If you want, I could go to the reception with you."

CHAPTER SIX

TOM AND CATHERINE'S wedding reception was being held at a swank hotel restaurant in the financial district. Since she had no time or money to buy something new, Margo wore the same red dress that she'd bought for her high school reunion last spring. Robert picked her up at the bistro and when he walked in dressed in a perfectly elegant black suit and gray tie, she definitely felt the earth move. But it wasn't the sort of tremor that any Richter scale could measure.

She took a deep breath as she gathered her cashmere scarf and handbag. She knew Robert had offered to escort her out of kindness—the same reason he'd agreed to help her with the accounting. But her insides still felt as if she was out on a date.

"This is so nice of you," she said, letting him take her arm as he walked her to his car.

"I'm the lucky one," he assured her politely.

Well, maybe there was more than good manners

behind his answer. From the widening of his eyes and the swift intake of his breath, Margo guessed he liked the way she looked in her dress.

As they drove along Market Street toward the bay, she allowed herself to speculate. What if this *were* a date? A *real* first date? If so, it would be one of the weirdest on record, since they were attending her ex-husband's wedding reception. And her kids would be there.

"So." Robert pulled his tie out from his throat. "What should I expect?"

"I'm not really sure." She didn't know how many guests had been invited or what the program was. Would there be speeches? A wedding cake? She gulped. "I didn't bring a gift. I didn't even think of it."

Robert gave her a rueful smile. "That's probably okay. You could always send something later."

"Yeah." She supposed she should. But she didn't feel like buying Tom and Catherine a gift. She didn't feel like going to this wedding, either. If it wasn't for the kids, she certainly wouldn't. She did wish Tom well, but she didn't want to witness this new start of his. There was a limit to how generous a woman could feel toward a man who had cheated on her and abandoned her. At some point, he should have had to suffer for that.

Instead, he was getting married. Wasn't that just lovely?

They parked at Embarcadero Center, and Robert courteously held her elbow as they made their way from the car to the building. In the elevator, Margo's nerves bubbled like the champagne she was sure she'd be drinking in just a few moments.

She glanced at Robert, whose hands were clasped in front of him. He was standing with his weight on his heels, his gaze fixed on the lighted numbers above the elevator door. He didn't look nervous or uncomfortable and she wondered what he must be thinking.

Probably, he was wishing he was anywhere but here right now. Like she was.

The elevator doors opened and before she could suggest they bolt and go for fish and chips on the wharf, Robert's hand was on her elbow again.

The restaurant offered a 360-degree panorama of the city and the bay, and when they first walked in, all Margo could do was stare. While Robert took her wrap to the coat check, a waiter stepped forward to hand her the expected glass of champagne.

About fifty elegantly dressed guests circulated in the room, and at first perusal, Margo didn't recognize any of them. Then her children came running for her, just as Robert returned.

"Mom!" Peter wrapped his arms around her waist and Ellie was right behind him. Margo kissed them both, careful not to get lipstick on their cheeks, then stepped back for inspection.

It seemed Ellie's old pink shoes had not been an issue. She was outfitted in a brand-new dress, along with matching shoes. Peter wore an adorable little suit and a plaid bow tie.

"Kids, I'd like you to meet a new friend of mine, Mr. Brookman. Robert, these are my children, Ellie and Peter."

Though Robert gave them a warm smile, both kids looked at him suspiciously. Margo wondered if she'd been wise to spring a new man on them at such an emotionally charged event. To distract them, she brushed a hand over Peter's jacket, then Ellie's dress. "You guys look terrific. Did your father take you shopping?"

"Catherine did. We went this morning." Ellie's eyes glowed. "And then we went to the hairdresser's. And got our nails painted." She touched a hand to the springy curls that had been artfully arranged on top of her head.

Margo's chest tightened. She couldn't remember when she'd last had time to shop with Ellie. And yet Catherine had made time on her wedding day. And she'd picked out such nice things… Ellie had never looked prettier.

Margo forced a smile and tried to turn her thoughts in a positive direction. *I should be happy for Ellie.*

But she didn't feel happy. She felt sick.

And then she saw Catherine, attached to Tom's side as if with Krazy Glue. She was lovely and elegant, with thick, chestnut hair and smooth, ivory skin. She was wearing a blush-colored suit, matching shoes and a lacy blouse.

Suddenly Margo's dress, which she'd once considered sexy and sleek, felt loud, loud, loud.

She checked out the proud groom next. Tom looked happy and satisfied and she had to turn away. "Catherine?" Her voice seemed to come from far away. "It's nice to finally meet you."

She'd never uttered words that were less sincere. She felt miserable and insecure and totally extraneous. And then someone took her hand and squeezed it reassuringly.

Robert. She'd almost forgotten about him.

"Hi, I'm a friend of Margo's." He introduced himself to her ex and his new wife and offered the appropriate congratulations, all the while giving her a lifeline to grasp until she finally found her composure again.

"What do you do, Robert?" There was no edge to Tom's question, just polite interest.

He really is over me, Margo realized. *Was she completely over him, too?*

Tough question. In all honesty, she had to admit that she didn't think it was because Catherine had taken Margo's place with Tom. What made this so difficult were the children. Was there something wrong with her that she found it so hard to share them? That she wanted them with her all the time?

"I'm in banking." Robert said in answer to Tom's question.

Margo noticed how he adjusted his tie, a slight betrayal of tension as he delivered his vague response. She'd sensed before that his unemployed status was a big issue with him.

"It looks like that man over there is trying to get your attention," she told Tom, in order to distract him from asking more questions.

Tom glanced over his shoulder, then turned to Catherine. "Sweetheart, we should be starting dinner shortly."

"Of course." Catherine smiled at Margo. "We've sat you with an old friend of yours." She pointed out a table not far from where they were standing. A couple was already sitting there, drinks in hand. "I believe you know my boss, Henry Kovatch and his wife, Nancy?"

Sure. Good old Henry, who'd hooked these two up in the first place. Margo had been hoping to be seated with Ellie and Peter, but instead she watched despondently as Tom and Catherine led her children to the head table.

"God, this sucks."

Robert lowered his head and spoke just inches from her ear. "Want to leave?"

A delicious shiver loosened the tension in her shoulders. "Yes."

He looked surprised.

"But I can't." She took his hand. "Come with me and I'll introduce you to Henry and Nancy."

"I can hardly wait," Robert replied in a tone that told her he was lying. Yet, he followed just the same.

Days Unemployed: 6

ROBERT WAS SURPRISED to find that he liked Henry and Nancy Kovatch. They'd been married for twelve years and had children the same ages as Margo and Tom's kids. As a couple, they seemed to be a pair of opposites, at least in appearance. Nancy was tall and slender, with a narrow face and short dark hair. Henry was pudgy, with a broad face and a receding hairline.

From the conversation it was clear that the couple had been close to Margo and Tom before their divorce. And that post-divorce Henry and

Nancy had spent more time with Tom than Margo. At any rate, they seemed to have a lot of catching up to do.

During the times when the conversation didn't involve him much, Robert watched Ellie and Peter at the head table. He noticed Peter drinking glass after glass of Coke, while Ellie seemed to be constantly engaging her new stepmother in conversation.

He was no psychologist, but to him the kids seemed to have adjusted well to their parents' divorce. They obviously liked their new stepmother. He shifted his attention back to Margo, who was just starting a story about her fifteen-year high school reunion, which she'd attended shortly after her separation from Tom.

Their conversation was interrupted when it came time for a toast from the head table. After that, salad was served and wineglasses topped up.

"So where is your bistro?" Nancy asked, spearing a shrimp from her salad plate. "Tom said it was in SOMA, but where exactly?"

Margo gave her the directions and Nancy requested a piece of paper from their server so she could write them down. "I'll have to come by one afternoon between shuffling the kids from place to place. I'll just have to see it to believe it."

Henry nodded. "We're still blown away that

you gave up law to open a restaurant. I can understand how working with Tom might have been difficult, but I could have made room for you at my firm." He caught Robert's eye. "Margo was a brilliant family law lawyer. She could get the most intractable couple to sit down at the bargaining table and be reasonable."

Margo said nothing, just smiled, but Robert could see the tension straining her lips. He hadn't realized she'd worked in family law. Now her decision to start her own bistro didn't seem quite so crazy. Maybe dealing with divorcing couples every day had become too difficult for her once she'd found herself in a similar situation.

"Margo's pretty talented in the kitchen, too," he said. "If you do go to the bistro, Nancy, you should try to make it for lunch. Her soups are incomparable."

"Margo always was a good cook," Henry allowed.

Robert felt a buzzing near his heart. He put his hand over his BlackBerry, which was safely ensconced in the breast pocket of his dinner jacket. "Excuse me a minute."

The conversation continued behind him as he made his way to the men's washrooms. At this hour on a Saturday night it didn't seem likely that this call could be about a job prospect, but he didn't want to chance it.

A glance at the call display, however, revealed a very familiar number. "Belinda?"

"It's Andrew."

Robert sank back against the washroom wall.

"You didn't come to my party."

He should have called. Belinda had said she didn't want him to, but he should have explained why he couldn't go. "Did you have fun, buddy? Did your mom get you that chocolate cake?"

"I want to go fishing, Robert. You said—"

There was a clattering sound, then in the background Robert heard Belinda say, "Go to your room, please. I'll be there in a minute to talk to you." A second pause, then, "Robert?"

"Hey, Belinda." He rubbed a hand over his head, preparing himself for an onslaught.

"Did Andrew call you, or did you phone him?"

Robert didn't want to rat on the poor kid. "Does it really matter? Frankly, I'm not so sure that we're handling this situation correctly. I think—"

"Stop right there. This isn't easy for me, either. You don't know the pressure I'm under. But Dean is trying to be a father to Andrew and I love Dean and I have to make it work."

"I get that. But couldn't Andrew and I—"

"No, Robert. No." Belinda let out a long, tired

sigh. "Please don't phone Andrew again. Please, please give me a chance to sort this out."

"You've had eight months." That came out sounding too harsh. He softened his tone. "Andrew still seems to miss me. And I miss him, too. I don't see what it would hurt—"

"Well, it is hurting, okay?" she said, interrupting him again. "For your information, Andrew is sobbing in his room right now. I can hear him from here."

"Oh, Belinda…"

"Just don't call again, okay? Please, don't call again."

Before he could say anything, she disconnected. Robert stared at his phone a moment, then closed it and slipped it back into his pocket. He hoped Belinda knew what she was doing. Right now, he had his doubts.

Another guest came into the washroom and held the door open for him. Robert stepped out into the restaurant, but hesitated before rejoining his table.

He could see Margo from here. She was listening to something Henry was saying. Listening and smiling. He felt the urge to be closer to her. An urge he'd been feeling since the first time he saw her.

This situation is different, he assured himself,

as he started moving forward. But even as he slipped back into the chair he'd vacated ten minutes ago, he felt Ellie watching him and he couldn't help but worry that he was about to make another major mistake.

AFTER THE WEDDING CAKE had been cut and served, Margo wished Tom and Catherine the best, then gathered her children to take them home. The happy couple were leaving on their honeymoon in the morning—a quick two-day jaunt to Palm Springs since Tom didn't want to book off too much vacation time.

That Tom, he was such a romantic. But that was Catherine's problem now, not hers.

Robert carried Peter to the car for her. Even Ellie stumbled with exhaustion a few times. They'd had quite a weekend, her kids, but they'd all survived, thank goodness.

Margo knew that in her case, she had Robert to thank for helping the evening pass so smoothly. Once they were in his car, driving home, both children quickly nodded off to sleep. Margo glanced back at them, then touched Robert's arm.

"I don't think a lifetime supply of soup and scones would be enough to repay you for what you did tonight. I couldn't have made it through that evening on my own."

He glanced her way. "You're stronger than you think. You would have been fine."

Would she have? Maybe. Margo sighed, and sank a little more deeply into her seat. Outside her window, a kaleidoscope of lights, buildings and cars passed in a blur. For the first time all night she felt at peace. Was it because she had her children back in her care?

Or was it the man beside her?

Once they were home, Robert parked out front of the bistro, then helped carry her children up to their bedrooms. He left her tucking them in, not giving her time to say more than a whispered good-night and another brief thank-you.

Margo had kicked her heels off at the front door. Now, as she pulled the quilt up around Ellie's shoulders, she fought the urge to crawl into bed next to her daughter. She was the one who needed comfort, not Ellie. And that wasn't right. She was the mother. She was supposed to be strong for her children, not the other way around.

As Margo stood to leave, Ellie's hand crept out from the covers and tugged on the hem of her dress.

"You looked pretty tonight, Mommy."

Oh, baby. "So did you, sweetheart. You and Catherine found the perfect dress. And your hair was just lovely."

"I told you Catherine was nice. Did you like her, too?"

Margo swallowed. "I did."

"Good." Ellie's voice faded. She sighed and drifted back to sleep. Margo stood watching her for several minutes, before heading for her own bed.

CHAPTER SEVEN

Days Unemployed: 7

THE CALL FROM ANDREW spooked Robert, to the point that on Sunday he decided he couldn't help Margo with her accounting anymore. He couldn't go back to the bistro, period. He tried phoning her. His plan was to beg off with the excuse that he was just too busy. But when the answering machine kicked in, he hung up.

He couldn't tell Margo he was leaving her in the lurch on a machine. Yet every time he tried to reach her, he got the damn recording.

On Monday he tried to focus on his job search and just forget about her. Some business happened to take him by the bistro. He checked out the soup of the day, almost gave in, then gathered his strength and walked on by.

On Tuesday he went in.

He couldn't say why he did this. It wasn't

planned and it certainly wasn't smart. It was sort of like having a craving for potato chips, deciding it would be better to forgo all that extra fat and salt and then finding yourself sitting on the sofa with the bag open in your hands.

He didn't remember making the conscious decision to go to Margo's. Couldn't remember the details of the walk that had taken him there. But when he stepped into the open door and the sight of her behind the counter and the wafting aroma of fresh, homemade soup, hit him, he knew he'd come to the right place.

His usual table was free and he claimed it with relief. Instead of ordering something immediately, he opened that day's newspaper, then sat back and watched Margo.

She smiled at every customer. And she seemed to know many of them by name. The customers' faces brightened after talking to Margo, he noticed.

Cooking wasn't her only gift.

During a lull in business, she came to him with a bowl of soup and a scone. He waited for her to ask him where he'd been, but she didn't.

"How's the job search going?"

He held out a hand. "Don't ask."

"Sorry to hear that. I thought maybe you'd found something…."

That would have explained why he hadn't shown up on Monday as he'd promised to. But he didn't have a good reason for that. At least not one that he could tell her.

He nodded at the food she'd brought him. "When I'm done with this, would it be a good time for me to keep working on those cash flow statements?"

Her cheeks pinkened. "You don't need to do that. You've already helped enough. With the books and…other things."

She was thinking of their sort-of-date on Saturday night. But he didn't see how that could count as a favor. He'd enjoyed himself. Enjoyed being with her and watching her with her kids and just…being with her.

"You'd be doing me a favor by letting me help. Before I'm reduced to watching daytime television." He couldn't believe he was practically begging her to do something he'd decided he absolutely wanted no part of. He tensed as she considered the offer—then relaxed when she slowly nodded.

"If you're *sure*…"

"I am." And he was. Sure he was being a total idiot.

Tuesday's Soup of the Day:
Corny Cauliflower

HE WAS BACK. After showing Robert up to her apartment, Margo couldn't believe how light-footed she suddenly felt. No customer's request was too much trouble. Every rambunctious child was cute, rather than annoying.

She took him a cup of coffee and a brownie around three. When she returned from picking up the kids from school, he was just finishing for the day.

"How about a coffee for the road?"

He accepted the offer and she filled an extra-large-sized cup for him as her kids perched on their stools for their usual after-school snack. Peter didn't pay much attention to Robert, but Margo noticed Ellie give him a couple of studied looks.

"Robert's helping me with the business side of running the bistro. Doing the accounting and preparing the statements I need for the bank."

Peter ignored the information, but Ellie seemed interested. "Don't you have to go to work in the day? My dad doesn't come home until dinnertime. Sometimes later."

Robert focused on pressing a lid onto his coffee cup as he answered. "I'm between jobs right now."

"Do you have kids?"

His jaw muscle tightened. "No."

Margo was a little surprised at his brusque answers. The other night she'd gotten the impression that Robert liked kids.

Peter downed the last of his juice. "I'm still thirsty."

For the first time there was a flicker of interest in Robert's eyes as he glanced at her son, but it disappeared quickly. "I'll catch you tomorrow," he said to Margo, before taking off without a word of goodbye to the kids.

"He doesn't like us," Ellie said.

Margo frowned. "That's crazy. How could anyone not like you guys?" She gave them both a hug and was about to usher them upstairs to start on their homework when her cell phone rang.

She whipped the phone out of her apron with a premonition of trouble. Only a week ago Tom had called to tell her about his wedding. What was it going to be this time?

Leaving Em behind the counter, Margo took the call in the kitchen, her back resting against the door to the industrial-sized refrigerator.

"Margo speaking."

"This is Ruth Bigsby, Margo. How are you?"

Peter's first-grade teacher. "Fine, thanks. Is Peter having trouble at school?"

"No, no, he's doing fine. I didn't mean to alarm

you by calling. But there is a small concern I wanted to mention."

"Yes?" Small concern. How small? This was probably something to do with Tom's wedding and the recent upheaval in all their lives. Margo hadn't seen much change in Peter at home, but maybe he'd been acting out in class.

"Peter's been excusing himself to go to the bathroom quite frequently, lately."

"Oh?" Margo didn't see the problem. "Peter drinks a lot of water."

"Yes, he keeps his water bottle at his desk and usually I have no problem with that, but it has struck me as excessive lately and I thought I should tell you. In case you wanted to take him to see his doctor."

Pull her son out of school, leave Em short-handed at the bistro and go to the doctor's office because her son liked to drink water? "Well, thanks, Ruth. I appreciate that you're worried about Peter."

Margo disconnected the call, then hustled the kids up to the apartment. "I'll be back soon," she told Em, but Ellie needed help with a research project and Margo found herself entangled on the World Wide Web trying to suss out facts on ant colonies.

At five, when the staff changeover occurred, she

ran downstairs to make sure all was well. She found Sandy covering for Edward again.

What was with that guy? When he'd applied for the job he'd seemed almost desperate for the extra income. And for the first while he'd been such a good worker. She'd have to have a more serious talk with him, and soon, Margo realized.

But not tonight. She was already running late as it was, and Nora was planning to stop by for a coffee later. She was bringing a new friend with her tonight, an installation artist named Selena Milano. Margo didn't quite know what an installation artist was. She supposed she would find out later.

Margo pulled a lasagna from the freezer for dinner and chopped fresh veggies for Ellie and Peter to snack on in the meantime. Dinner was late—but then she'd never been known for serving it on schedule. Earlier she'd been busy baking a lemon tart for Nora and Selena. She'd set it aside to cool and now she placed it on a tray, along with serving plates and forks.

To expedite bedtime she decided to forgo baths this one time. As was becoming usual, Peter fell asleep before she finished the Spider-Man adventure he'd chosen as his bedtime story. She went to Ellie's room.

"I read your report, honey. You did a terrific job."

Ellie nodded without looking up from the first Harry Potter book. She was rereading the entire series in anticipation of the latest movie release.

Margo bent to kiss her cheek. "I'm going downstairs to have coffee with my friends. I've got the monitor with me, so just shout if you or your brother need anything."

"We'll be fine, Mom." Ellie spoke again without raising her head.

Loving the fact that her daughter could get that engrossed in a book, Margo hurried down the stairs. The first thing she saw as she stepped out of the kitchen was Edward—talking to a group of girls at a table for four. She went behind the counter to confer with Sandy.

"When did he show up?"

Sandy rolled her eyes. "About ten minutes ago. Those girls are his friends. They came in with him."

Margo strode out from behind the counter and headed toward the table in question. As soon as she caught Edward's eye, he straightened and started backing away.

"Catch you later," he said. "The boss is getting mad at me."

As if to prove his point wrong, Margo smiled

at the girls, then turned to Edward. "Sandy has her hands full right now. Do you think you could help her?"

She would have hauled him into the kitchen for a serious chat, but Nora showed up then, with an exotic-looking woman who had to be Selena. Selena had short, dark curly hair, big brown eyes and a funky skirt and top that shouldn't have looked good together, yet did.

"Hey, Margo. Nice to see you." Nora gave her a hug. "This is my friend, Selena. She's working on a piece of art in front of our building right now."

Margo shook hands with the new arrival. Selena's skin felt a little gritty. The artist gave her an apologetic smile. "Sorry. I was working with papier-mâché today and I just couldn't scrub all that stuff off." She examined her right hand. "My nails are still a mess."

"Maybe so. But the rest of you looks great." Margo admired the way Selena's chunky turquoise jewelry complemented her coral top. Those were colors Margo simply couldn't wear, much as they suited the other woman.

"It's great to meet you, Selena, and I want to hear more about what you do, but first let me get us some coffees. Nora always has chai latte… What would you like?"

"Straight espresso for me, please." Selena swept an expert gaze around the bistro. "I just love your place. Good colors. Nice karma."

Margo liked her instantly.

Later, when they were all seated in the annex room, Margo found out that Selena had something very important in common with her and Nora. She was a single mom, too. Her son, Drew, was almost twelve.

"It's always been just the two of us," Selena said, almost smugly. "And that's the way I like it."

"No joint-custody issues," Margo noted. "That must be nice." Still, despite the headaches of coordinating schedules with Tom, she was glad that her children had a father in their lives. She knew Nora felt the lack for her son, Danny, even if Selena did not.

"So, tell us about the wedding reception." Nora glanced at Selena. "Margo's ex got remarried last Saturday and she was invited."

"Oh." Selena's face softened with sympathy. "Was that tough?"

"Not as bad as I thought it would be. The venue was amazing. I took a card from the restaurant." Margo passed it to Nora. "I thought your sister might be interested, for her wedding."

"Thanks. I'll be sure to give this to Suzanne. But tell us more about the night."

"Ellie and Peter looked adorable. And they seemed fine. I think they actually had a pretty good time."

"What's the new stepmom like?" Nora asked.

"Very attractive and elegant." Margo grimaced. "Not only is she nice-looking but I think she may actually be a genuinely nice person."

"That's terrible," Selena said.

Margo laughed. Selena obviously got it. "I know. I really wanted to dislike her. But now I don't even get that small satisfaction."

"So now are you wishing you'd taken my advice and asked a date to the reception?" Nora wondered.

"Actually…"

"She did take someone!" Selena raised her espresso cup in salute. "Way to go, sister!"

Margo couldn't help but grin.

"Was it the banker? Robert? Oh, I can't believe this—Margo's finally gone on a date!"

"Don't make me sound like such a loser, Nora. Only…maybe I am. Because it wasn't really a date. I told Robert about the ceremony and he offered to go with me for moral support."

"He *volunteered* to go to your ex's wedding?" Nora shook her head. "I didn't think they made guys that nice anymore."

"I'm not sure they *ever* made them that nice."

Selena picked up the knife Margo had set next to the tart. "Is anyone else hungry? Because I can't look at this beautiful thing another second longer without biting into it."

"Dive in," Margo encouraged her. "And to tell you the truth, I can't figure Robert's motives out. He's been helping me with the accounting, besides going to that reception with me."

"You want to know his motives?" Selena passed a plate to Margo. "That's easy. He wants to sleep with you."

Just the suggestion gave her a little buzz. She tried to blame the feeling on too much espresso in her double mocha tonight. "No way. We've been alone several times. And he's never even tried to kiss me."

"Really?"

Nora looked surprised and Margo realized she'd just made a rather pathetic admission. She and Robert were both unattached singles, about the same age, who'd been spending lots of time together lately. Why *hadn't* he tried to kiss her?

"The theory still holds," Selena insisted. "It's just that Robert hasn't yet realized that he wants to sleep with you. Or perhaps he has, and he's fighting the attraction for some reason."

"Maybe he's scared off by the fact that I have two kids." Margo thought about how stilted he'd been that afternoon when he was at the counter with Ellie and Peter. That was it, she decided, as disappointment tightened around her chest. Robert didn't like children.

"Could be," Nora allowed. "He sure seemed to back off the other night when he saw the photographs of Danny, Peter and Ellie."

"That's right. He did." Margo thought about how happy she'd felt this afternoon when he'd showed up again after a couple days away. But if he didn't like kids… Well. He definitely wasn't the right guy for her, no matter how nice he seemed to be.

"Hey, I almost forgot." Nora placed a paper bag on the table. "I bought you a present."

Margo pulled out a mug. Spelled on the side was a motto that seemed very appropriate for her life right now. *Wake Up and Smell the Coffee.*

"It made me think of you," Nora said. "Of us. That it's time to start broadening our horizons."

"You talking about men?" Selena asked.

Margo grinned, her mood lightening. No doubt about it. She liked Selena. "That's right."

"Well, as long as we keep things fun and casual, I'm all for men. Can I join the club?"

Margo exchanged glances with Nora. "Club?"

"The Singles With Kids club," Selena elaborated.

"That sounds like us, all right." Nora cut three new slices of the tart, then slid one onto each of their plates.

"Dig in, everyone." As she picked up her fork, Margo felt comforted. It was a crazy world out there for a single woman with young children to raise. But at least she wasn't alone.

CHAPTER EIGHT

Days Unemployed: 11

THE NEXT MORNING Robert made a new rule for himself. He would go to Margo's only if the agenda was all business. He'd buy lunch, update his job search queries, then prepare the cash flow statement for Margo. That was all. He wouldn't allow himself to spend any time alone with her. Above all, he would leave the bistro before her children returned home from school.

Yesterday had been a close call. It was obvious that Ellie was already suspicious of his role in her mother's life.

As for Peter… Robert frowned. The young boy was the physical opposite of Andrew, blond and slight rather than stocky and dark, but he had that same trusting light in his eyes that had drawn Robert to Belinda's son. He had to keep his distance from those kids.

The real problem here, of course, was Margo.

There was a sparkle about the woman. The sincerity in her smile was difficult to resist. As he'd watched her serve her male customers, he'd wondered why they didn't all fall instantly in love with her.

Like he had? No. He wasn't in love with Margo. Just a little bit infatuated. Soon, the right job opportunity would present itself and then he'd be out of temptation's way. Once he was working his usual long hours in the financial district, he'd forget all about Margo's Bistro. It was just because he had so much idle time on his hands that he couldn't seem to stay away from her right now.

After a workout and shower at the gym, Robert drove to the bistro. Margo served him a coffee and a muffin, before taking him up to the apartment to work on the books. At noon she brought his lunch on a tray and then left him alone to eat it.

So far his plan to spend as little time with her as possible was working.

Possibly too well.

He ate quickly, resisting with effort the temptation to go downstairs and see if she had any time to talk. Instead, he checked in with his headhunter and returned a few calls.

Then back to the cash flow statements. No matter how he tried to juggle the numbers, though, he couldn't get the result he wanted, the results Margo needed.

An hour later, he accepted the inevitable and printed off the statements. Glancing at his watch, he saw he'd finished just in time. He still had a half hour before Margo went to pick up the kids from school. He wanted to be long gone by the time they arrived home.

He tracked Margo down in the kitchen as she was pulling a tray of muffins from the oven. "Hey. Just wanted to let you know that I'm finished."

She swiveled to face him, the hot tray still in her hands. Her cheeks were flushed and she was smiling. She looked very pretty.

"Would you like to test one of these before you go?"

He forced his eyes from her face to the muffins. "Are those the same kind you made last week?"

"I've modified the recipe a little. They should be better."

He waited as she dumped the steaming-hot muffins out onto a clean cloth.

"Help yourself."

He broke a corner off one of them and popped it into his mouth. His taste buds were immediately impressed. "Wow, this is lots better. Here— you try."

Robert broke off another piece and fed it to her.

Her lips parted. He felt the flick of her tongue on his finger. For a moment their eyes connected. Then they both glanced away.

Margo chewed, then judged the results. "The texture is much better. Flavor, too. Not bad."

"Better than that. I've never tasted anything like this."

"Yes…but…" She took a second taste, then frowned. "I don't know. I'm still missing something."

"Are you sure?" Robert popped a bigger piece into his mouth. "I think they're perfect the way they are."

"Maybe." Margo jotted a few comments in her notebook. When she set down the pen, she gave him a hopeful look. "So the cash flow statement is ready for the bank?"

He couldn't look at her as he nodded. "I printed it out for you and left it on the desk upstairs."

"That's great. But…is something wrong?"

"Margo, when the bank sees those cash flow projections, they're going to be concerned. As they should be."

He forced himself to look her square in the eyes. She stiffened her shoulders. "Why? What's wrong?"

"You're running out of money."

"The summer months are coming. I'm expecting an increase in business…."

"Revenue generation isn't the problem. This place is leaking cash."

Her face whitened.

"I'm sorry to be the one to deliver the bad news."

"But we're almost always busy. We only have a few slow times during the day."

"The problem lies with your expenses. They're just too high. You need to manage your staff more efficiently. Improve your product pricing and inventory control."

Margo sighed. "I know I haven't been focusing on the business end enough. But there's never enough time to study all those reports. Besides, numbers were never my strong suit."

Robert hesitated. Today was supposed to be the last time he helped Margo with her accounting. But how could he deliver bad news like this, then walk away?

He was no expert on managing restaurants. But he could help her. He knew that he could.

"Let me see what I can do. I can juggle some numbers and do a little analysis. Maybe I can help you figure out what you need to change in order to make this business profitable."

She looked hopeful and worried at the same

time. "But do you have time? I know you're searching for a new job. You'll probably be offered something really soon."

He wished. "I do have a couple interviews lined up for Friday and next week."

"Well, that's great. Congratulations." He could tell she was making an effort to be happy for him.

"Yeah. We'll see how it goes. But in the meantime, I've still got some extra time." He'd *make* the time to help her. He checked his watch and saw that it was almost four.

"Aren't you late to pick up your kids?"

"They spend Wednesday nights with their father." Margo tucked a strand of hair behind her ear.

Robert felt his heart take on a heavy, pounding rhythm. His mouth went a little dry. *Leave,* he told himself, but it was the last thing he wanted to do. "Feel like going for a walk and maybe grabbing a bite to eat?"

He didn't think it was his imagination that Margo's face brightened.

"I'm sure Em won't mind being on her own for an hour until my evening staff arrives. Hang on and I'll grab my purse."

Five minutes later, they were strolling down the street. Margo had slipped a little jean jacket over her pink T-shirt. He had a hard time looking anywhere but at her.

"This was such a good idea." Margo grinned like a kid who'd snuck out of school early and was thrilled at the unexpected freedom. "I don't get out enough. Back when I worked in an office ten hours a day, I used to dream of having the freedom to roam the streets during daylight."

Robert stepped aside to make room for a teenager with purple hair and earphones, walking two dogs on a tandem leash.

"Look at all this life." She waved her arm in a sweeping gesture meant to encompass everything on the block.

Obligingly, Robert looked. He saw lovers sitting at an outdoor café, a kid on Rollerblades—surely not yet twenty—carrying a fat briefcase. Two women, arms linked, window-shopping in front of an art gallery and arguing about whether or not they should step inside.

"Let's go this way," Margo said as she grabbed his arm and pulled him around a corner.

The feeling of being tugged by a lively, sparkly eyed Margo was not at all unpleasant. "Any particular reason?"

She looked at him as if he was brain dead. "Don't you want to go to the Yerba Buena Gardens? Whenever I go for a long walk in SOMA, I always head there."

He cocked his head. "I've only lived here a year, but I do think I remember driving by—"

"Driving? That's terrible." She started pulling harder on his arm. "You have got so much to see, Robert."

He hurried along with her, caught on the current of her enthusiasm. Yes. He definitely had that feeling. He had so much to see.

ONCE THEY REACHED the gardens, Margo took Robert to all her favorite places. She started with the twenty-foot falling water memorial to Martin Luther King and ended up at the carousel, where she tried to cajole him into climbing on one of the painted ponies. "Pleassse. It'll be so much fun."

Smiling, he shook his head. "You go. I'll watch."

She kept a grip on his hand. "You come, too."

But he let her hand slip away, and she found herself alone in the line.

"Go on," Robert mouthed, and she decided she would.

She picked one of the horses on the outer circle and when the music started and the carousel began to rotate, she couldn't help but laugh for the sheer fun of it.

Every time she circled by him, Robert smiled and his eyes never seemed to leave her. When the ride was over, he was right at the exit, waiting for her.

This time it was *him* pulling *her* to a quiet spot under a tree. He swung her around so she was facing him, then he put both hands on her waist and brought her in close for a kiss.

The moment their mouths met she felt a connection that sizzled through her body, all the way to her toes. When he pulled away for an instant she thought he whispered, "Wow," but she couldn't be sure.

They kissed again, more deeply, and when he cupped her face with his hands, she felt… treasured. He eased back a little, let his mouth linger on hers, then released her.

She put a hand on his shoulder. Dizzy from the carousel? Or the kiss? Both had been wonderful, but no question which she'd preferred.

"You're good at that, Robert."

"*We're* good at that." He looked bothered, suddenly, as if sharing a great kiss wasn't a terrific thing.

Maybe, for him, it happened all the time. "That woman you moved to San Francisco for? She must have been special."

"I thought so at the time."

"I know how that feels. What happened?"

"She met someone new. Someone from work. They're living together now."

"Funny how some people step from one relationship straight into another." That was what Tom had done, too. "I think it's better to adjust to being alone first, but I guess some people are afraid of being on their own."

Robert put his hands on either side of her face again. "When your marriage ended, did being alone frighten you?"

"For a short time, yes. Until I figured out that it's actually less lonely living without a man, than living with one who doesn't love you."

Robert stared at her deeply. "I don't get it."

"Why it's hard to live with someone who doesn't love you?"

"No. How someone could not love you. What was the matter with your ex, Margo? If you'd been my wife, and if Ellie and Peter were my kids, I'd be counting my blessings."

Lord, it did her soul good to hear those words. She'd never had self-esteem problems before. But when she'd found out Tom was having an affair, and then when he'd left her, she'd found herself battling self-doubt.

"I'm not much of a housekeeper, Robert. Our house was always full of friends, neighbors, the children's playmates. It was noisy and chaotic and never the same one day to the next. Tom hated that."

"What about you? What did you hate?"

She thought for a moment. "That nothing I did ever made him happy. That when I tried to share an experience that had thrilled me, he didn't care."

Robert swallowed. "I just thought of another reason someone might jump from one relationship directly into another."

"Yes."

"It could be a simple matter of timing. When you meet the right person, you just know."

He kissed her again, and Margo was even more dazed than she had been the first time. They didn't talk much after that and Margo was glad. Inside she felt all giddy and happy, but the feelings were tender and she knew they'd fall apart all too easily.

"I need to return to the bistro before closing."

They held hands all the way back, but Robert didn't kiss her again. Instead he brushed a hand over her cheek and told her he'd see her the next day.

Margo waited a minute before stepping inside.

She'd started falling for Robert from that first day when he'd hogged the table in the back corner…but their kiss had sealed things. It suggested a connection that was deeper than anything she'd experienced before. And as much as that excited her…it also scared her to death.

In her marriage, she'd laid her heart bare, but Tom had never known what to do with the gift. If she was going to love again—and that was a big if—she was going to proceed with extreme caution.

Margo took a deep breath, then finally went inside. She looked around at the warmth and creative energy of her restaurant. Lots of tables were full now. Inviting scents permeated the air and the background music was subtle, but inviting.

Everything was going great. All she had to do was push Robert's financial verdict to the back of her mind, and she'd believe that this was a successful venture.

She spied Sandy behind the counter and looked around for Edward. He was standing by that table of girls again. When he spotted her, he hung his head guiltily, then made his way to the kitchen. Margo glanced at Sandy, who shrugged her shoulders, then continued steaming milk.

Margo slipped past the lineup of customers and joined Sandy behind the counter. "How's it going? Can I help?"

"We could use some more poppy-seed cake if you have any. I sent Edward for some about ten minutes ago, but—"

"Yes. I saw how that worked out. I'll go get it for you." Margo saw no sign of Edward in the kitchen. She pulled out the cake, took it out front for Sandy, then went looking for Edward again.

She noticed his jacket was missing from the hook by the back door. That was when she saw the note by the phone.

Sorry, had to leave early. Also, someone from the bank called, just before six. They said to remind you about those reports. They'd like to see them as soon as possible.

CHAPTER NINE

Days Unemployed: 12

THE NEXT MORNING Robert had to acknowledge that his plan had failed. He had not managed to contain his involvement with Margo as easily as he had hoped. Not only had he committed himself to helping her further with her business, but he'd asked her out.

And he'd kissed her.

That kiss had kept him up for an hour last night and had followed him into his dreams.

Keeping his distance from Margo was now patently impossible. All he could try to do now, to mitigate the potential fallout, was to avoid any close involvement with her children.

But that afternoon his latest resolution was put to the test. He'd spent several hours working on cost management analysis alone in Margo's apartment. When the time came to leave, he went to say goodbye and found Margo alone behind the counter.

"Where's Em?"

"Her daughter is sick and she had to go home."

"But don't you have to pick up your kids?"

She gave him a pleading look. "Could you go for me?"

Oh, no. He wasn't going to walk her children home from school. "You go. I'll stay here and take care of things while you're gone."

"Robert, I don't have enough time to show you how to work the cash register, let alone the Marzocco."

He took one look at the imposing red espresso machine and knew he'd been licked. "Okay. Fine. I'll go get them."

She gave him the directions to the school, and he jogged the whole way so he'd get there in time. He found Peter waiting on the corner Margo had described.

"Ellie's not here." Peter sighed. "She's always slow."

He didn't seem surprised that Robert, and not his mother, had come to pick him up. Soon Robert found out why.

"Are you Mommy's new boyfriend? Ellie says you are. She says you're going to get married and I'll have to wear my suit again."

Robert scratched his head. "Want to play on the jungle gym, Peter?"

Peter's face broke out in a smile, his question forgotten. *Little boys were so easy to distract.* But Robert guessed the sister wouldn't be as easy. When Ellie did show up, about ten minutes later, he took an offensive approach. "Let's play twenty questions. Do you guys know that game?"

They did and so Robert thought of a word, then challenged them to guess what he was thinking of. The game kept both kids occupied for the entire walk home. As they neared their street, Ellie zoomed in for the kill. "What is a saltshaker?"

"That's right, Ellie. I'm impressed." He held the bistro door open and both kids rushed inside. Ellie climbed onto one of the stools, while Peter rushed to use the washroom, then returned a minute later.

Robert watched as Peter downed a glass of juice in no time flat, then asked for another. No one seemed to find anything odd with how much the little boy drank, but he couldn't help but be suspicious. He wondered if he should say something to Margo or just mind his own business.

"Can I have a turn to think of a word now?" Peter asked.

Robert had been planning to leave, but he didn't have the heart to say no. He perched on a stool next to Ellie's and drank a coffee as he and Ellie posed questions to the little guy.

Though Margo was busy with customers, he saw her shoot a few approving looks his way. Those looks made him nervous. He hadn't meant to ingratiate himself with her kids. Quite the opposite.

"I should be going," he murmured to her, after both Peter and Ellie had each taken their turn at the game.

"Of course. Thanks so much for helping me out here. Again."

"No problem," he said, though it wasn't true. It was becoming a huge problem. Mostly because he kept enjoying himself so much. He started for the door, then his conscience forced him back. "Say…has Peter seen a doctor lately, by chance?"

Margo, usually a dervish of activity, stilled ominously. "Why?"

"I just notice that he seems to drink a lot. And go to the washroom. When I was about his age, I had a friend with the same symptoms. Turned out he had diabetes." Seeing Margo's stricken expression, he quickly backtracked. "Not that Peter has diabetes. I'm sure it's highly unlikely. It's just that you might want to get him checked."

Margo's face remained pale. "Peter's teacher phoned me yesterday with a similar comment about the washroom. I didn't think anything of it at the time. Diabetes didn't even occur to me."

He said nothing. If Peter's teacher had noticed the symptoms as well, then this was definitely something Margo needed to check on. She seemed to come to the same conclusion.

"I'll make an appointment with his doctor. Next week, maybe, once I've taken those cash flow statements to the bank."

"I don't think you should put it off."

She looked scared. Then she nodded. "Okay. I'll phone right now."

Friday's Soup of the Day: Alphabet Goop

MARGO TOLD HERSELF not to worry about Peter. Once a dentist's comment about inflamed lymph nodes on Ellie's neck had convinced her that Ellie had cancer. But Ellie had been fine. And Peter would be, too. The doctor's appointment was just a precaution.

An inconvenient precaution, as it turned out. She'd booked an appointment shortly after the lunch rush, but when the time came to pick Peter up from school, the bistro was insanely busy. She didn't see how Em would cope if she left. Just as she was about to phone the doctor's office and see if they could squeeze her in later, Robert showed up.

"The soup of the day sounds awful. If it didn't smell so good in here, I wouldn't order any."

Margo couldn't help feeling better at the sight of him. "My other customers don't seem to share your concern. We're almost sold out."

His eyebrows rose in alarm. "Then I guess I'd better get my order in right away." He leaned over the counter. "Didn't you have a doctor's appointment for Peter this afternoon?"

"I do. But I can't leave Em with all this." She gestured at the lineup of customers.

He took one look then calmly walked over to where she stood behind the counter and reached his arms around her neck. For one crazy moment she thought he was going to kiss her. Right there, in full view of the customers and Em. But all he did was lift the strap of her apron over her head.

"Go."

She stared into his eyes and thought the last thing she wanted to do right now was leave him. What she wanted was for him to put his arms around her again.

"Em will show me the ropes," Robert added. "Won't you, Em?"

"He's right, Margo. You better pick up that boy of yours and get him to the doctor."

Margo drove to the school and she and Peter headed straight to the clinic from there. Last night she'd arranged for Ellie to go to her friend Stephanie's house for a few hours after school so she wouldn't need to tag along to the appointment.

At the doctor's office Margo had to coax a urine sample from her son, then cross the hall to the lab where a tech pulled tubes of blood from her little boy's veins. Peter held her hand tightly and scrunched his eyes closed.

"It's okay, honey. Don't look at the needle, okay? Look at me and tell me what happened at school today."

All the while she was trying to distract Peter, Margo wondered how Robert was making out at the bistro. She shouldn't have let him talk her into leaving him there. It scared her how much she'd started to depend on him. She had to be more careful.

And it wasn't as if this was an emergency. Anyone could tell from looking at Peter that he was fine.

Once the blood test was over, she took Peter down to the car and on the long drive through rush-hour traffic thought about what to cook for dinner. Maybe she should invite Robert—to thank him for all the help he'd given her today. She could offer to pay him, too, but the wages she usually gave her employees would probably be an insult to an MBA.

As soon as she and Peter walked in the front door of the bistro, Robert whipped off his apron and tossed it behind the counter.

"What's wrong?" She glanced around. About half the tables were occupied, no one was waiting in line. Everything appeared to be under control.

"I'm thirsty," Peter said, tugging on her hand.

Robert gave him a pat on the back. "I've got a glass of water for you on the counter."

"But I want juice. And a cookie."

"Not just yet, pal." Robert turned to Margo. "Can we talk in the kitchen for a minute?"

She was getting really concerned now. Tension radiated from the man. Something was seriously out of kilter…only what? She followed him to the back room. "What is it, Robert?"

"The doctor's office called," he said without preamble. "You were supposed to go back there after the blood test. Now they want you to take Peter straight to the hospital."

MARGO'S FACE PALED and she started to shake. Robert did what felt right. He hugged her.

"Peter has diabetes. Doesn't he?"

Robert didn't want to be the one to tell her.

This shouldn't be happening to Margo and her kid. They were a nice family who'd been through a lot. She definitely had enough to deal with without this.

On the other hand, there was no denying the gravity he'd heard in the nurse's voice when he'd been talking to her on the phone. "It does sound that way," he admitted.

Margo eased out of his arms and swayed. "I've got to get going."

Robert didn't think it was a good idea for her to drive. "I'll take you."

She glanced out the open door to where a new customer waited at the counter. "I'll tell them you're closing," he said. "I can get this place cleared out in a few minutes."

She shook her head, then went to the sink and splashed her face with water. "I'm fine. Don't worry. It was a shock, but I'm okay now." She dried her face on a clean towel, then tossed it into the laundry bucket. "I'd consider it a big favor if you'd stay another fifteen minutes. Sandy should be here by then…I don't know about Edward." She grimaced. "He hasn't been very reliable lately."

"I'll stay," he said. "Don't worry, Em's been keeping me in line."

"Thank you."

THE LAST THING Margo wanted to do was alarm her son. So while she longed to scoop him into her arms and hold him close, she forced a smile instead.

"Hey, buddy. Looks like we have to go back and do a few more of those tests."

Peter had finished his water and had wandered to the counter to look at the baked goods on display. He scowled at her news. "Will they poke me again?"

Margo's heart twisted at those words. If Peter had diabetes, he was going to have to get used to having needles on a regular basis. She took his hand and gave him another smile. "Maybe, but there'll be some fun stuff, too."

"Yeah?" Peter looked at her hopefully.

Think fast, Margo. She couldn't. Maybe she'd find a little gift at the hospital shop to help distract him from whatever lay in wait for them. "It's a surprise. Come on, let's get going so we can get these tests over with."

"Can I take a cookie with me? I'm hungry."

From behind the counter, Robert shook his head. He'd put on the apron again, and she felt a flood of gratitude that he was here to help her today.

"Doctor's orders are for no food," Robert said.

Margo nodded her understanding, then bent to

face her son. "I'm sorry, Peter, but you're going to have to be patient about this."

Peter didn't cry often anymore, but at that moment he looked like he was going to. Then his hand went to his crotch in a telling little-boy mannerism.

"You need to go to the bathroom first?"

He nodded.

"Okay, honey. I'll wait right here."

Five minutes later they were back in San Francisco traffic, thankfully moving against the rushhour congestion. At the hospital, they were whisked through the admitting department and given instructions on where to go. Striding along the corridors at her son's pace, Margo recalled the last time she'd been to the E.R. here. She'd been afraid Peter had a broken ankle. It had turned out to be a sprain.

If only this visit could turn out to be a false alarm, too. Was it possible they'd made a mistake with the test? Read the results incorrectly? Gotten the results mixed up with someone else?

A nurse showed them into a communal room where the beds were separated by thick white curtains. She gave Peter a hospital gown to change into and he looked at Margo in dismay.

Poor little guy. Once the nurse had left, Margo helped him slip into the gown and about a minute after he'd crawled under the sheet provided, his doctor showed up.

Agata Shyleko had emigrated from Poland at least twenty years ago, but she still spoke with a slight accent. She was matronly looking, with kind hazel eyes and a warm, maternal smile.

"I'm glad you could get here so quickly. I've ordered a fasting glucose and two hour PC, which means Peter can't eat or drink anything except water for twelve hours."

Peter made a sound of dismay and Margo put her arm around him. "It's not so bad, hon. Most of that time you'll be sleeping."

"Depending on the test results, I'll be referring you to an internist." Dr. Shyleko smiled at Peter. "Don't worry. Dr. Green is a very nice man. He'll give you all the instructions you need on how to move forward."

She gestured for Margo to come talk to her privately.

"You think Peter has diabetes?" The blood was pounding in Margo's head so loudly, she could hardly hear the doctor's answer. But there was no mistaking the nod of her head.

"I know this is a shock for you, Margo, but it's important we get Peter started on treatment quickly, without alarming him unduly. He will need to learn to respect his disease, but I don't want him to be frightened of it. With good management, he can lead a fairly normal life."

Margo nodded because she couldn't speak without bursting into tears. Why did this have to happen to Peter? He was such a great kid. So fun and full of energy. Would that change now?

And how come she hadn't realized something was seriously wrong with him? She had to be the worst mother in the world. Lately, all she'd done was worry about her business and fantasize about Robert when she should have been focusing on her children. Even Peter's *teacher* had been paying closer attention to her child than she had.

"I need to call his father."

Dr. Shyleko nodded. "First let's get an IV line in. His blood sugar levels are quite high and I'd like to get him hydrated."

How ironic when all Peter did these days was drink. Margo took a deep breath, then returned to her son. In an effort to distract him, she suggested they play twenty questions. Peter was quickly drawn into the game, hardly noticing the nurse poking at his veins.

"When do I get my surprise?" he asked plaintively when it was over.

"Soon," she promised. "First I need to call your daddy."

One good thing about Tom, he was always levelheaded in emergency situations. He listened calmly as she explained everything that had happened that day, then told her to hang tight. He'd be at the hospital shortly.

Margo sat at Peter's bedside, trying to amuse him with a few picture books a nurse brought to them. She wished she'd thought to throw a few of Peter's favorite toys into a backpack.

As he'd promised, Tom arrived within the half hour. What surprised her though, was that Catherine was with him, carrying a duffel bag.

As soon as Peter saw the bag, he broke out smiling. "Did you bring Buzz Lightyear?"

"We sure did." Catherine set the bag on a chair, then pulled out Peter's favorite toy. There were other toys in the bag as well as clothes and books and even a Ziploc bag with a toothbrush and toothpaste inside.

Was it just luck that Catherine had known exactly what to pack? Or did she really know Peter that well?

"Hey, buddy, how are you doing?"

Margo moved so that Tom could give his son a hug. She tried not to bristle when Catherine moved closer, as well, and planted a kiss on Peter's forehead.

Who do you think you are? Margo wanted to ask her. How dare she step in here as if she were on par with Peter's *real* parents? Did she think she was impressing her new husband with this great show of maternal affection?

Margo took a deep breath. It wouldn't do Peter any good for her to get riled up about this. She turned to her ex. "Thanks for getting here so quickly."

"You can thank Catherine for that. She picked me up from work and drove me straight here."

"It was no problem," Catherine assured her. "What could be more important than Peter right now?"

Tom gave her a warm smile and patted her hand. When he turned his attention back to Margo, his expression was all business. "I'd like to speak to Peter's doctor."

Margo knew it was a reasonable request, and yet she found herself resenting it. *She'd* already spoken to Dr. Shyleko—and shared all the information with Tom over the phone. She shrugged and moved closer to her son, gently squeezing Catherine to the other end of the bed.

"How are you holding up?" Catherine laid a hand on her shoulder. "This must be hard on you."

Margo shifted a few inches away. "I'm fine."

Surprise, then disappointment registered in Tom's eyes at her curt response. What did he expect? That she and Catherine would become instant friends? Couldn't he see that his new wife's sympathy was too much for her to handle right now?

Aware that her emotions were spiraling out of control, Margo excused herself and went to find the washroom. As soon as she was in the corridor, her tears started to fall. No wonder Tom had looked at her that way. She was being a jerk. Worrying about her feelings when the only person who mattered right now was Peter.

In the washroom, Margo splashed water on her face for the second time that day and tried to pull herself together. The more people who cared about Peter, the better. That was the way she had to look at the situation. She ought to be grateful that Catherine had had the presence of mind to put together a bag of Peter's belongings for him.

She felt stronger when she slipped behind the curtain around her son's bed five minutes later. But her new composure didn't last long.

"I've spoken to the doctor," Tom said. "And it sounds like everything is under control. But where is Ellie?"

Margo's gaze flew to a clock on the wall, and immediately she felt sick to her stomach. She'd completely forgotten that she was supposed to pick her daughter up two hours ago.

CHAPTER TEN

IF THERE WERE an incompetent mother of the year award, Margo figured she'd be a shoe-in. Tom and Catherine had agreed to stay with Peter while she backtracked to Stephanie White's house to get her daughter.

On the way she called the Whites. Allan answered. "Don't worry. Ellie called home and one of your employees told her what was going on. When you didn't show up at the expected time, I wasn't surprised."

"Still, I'm sorry for the inconvenience."

"Not at all. I just hope your son is okay."

"He'll be fine," Margo assured him, wishing she could believe this herself. Right now she felt as if nothing was going to be right in her life ever again.

Fortunately Ellie wasn't upset about being kept waiting for so long. As soon as she'd scrambled into the car she asked, "Does Peter really have diabetes?"

"I'm afraid so." There was a child in Ellie's class who had the disease so Ellie had some comprehension of what her brother faced.

"Poor Peter." Ellie stared ahead grimly. "I'd hate to have to take those needles all the time."

"I know." And there'd be much more to contend with than just the insulin injections. This diagnosis was going to require close monitoring of Peter's diet and activity levels. She thought of all the cookies, muffins and scones they normally ate. His consumption of treats would have to be carefully controlled.

"Can we go see Peter now?"

"Yes. I just need to stop at the bistro first. While we're there, you should pack a bag. You may be spending the night at your father's."

Margo parked out front of the bistro, hoping to make it a quick stop. While Ellie grabbed her things, she would make sure Sandy was okay and that Edward wasn't goofing off again. But when she and Ellie walked in the front door, it was clear that even though it was two hours into his shift, Edward still hadn't shown up.

Robert was still there, though. He was behind the counter with Sandy, dealing efficiently with a small lineup of customers. He noticed her entrance right away and, without breaking stride, gave her a warm, concerned smile.

Margo stopped in her tracks, not sure of what she was feeling, only that it was powerful. She'd been half expecting chaos in the bistro. Instead, everything was running smoothly and it was because of Robert, she knew. Though he hadn't known her long, he was turning out to be someone she could really count on.

Which, in itself, was amazing enough. Yet when she thought of his kiss, and the weak, hungry feeling that had followed in its wake, she knew that with Robert, much more was possible.

If they dared to try.

But romance wasn't topping her priority list today.

Sandy passed a coffee to the last customer in line, then stepped out from behind the counter to clear tables. Margo went to help. "Looks like you've been busy."

"Yes. Thank goodness you're here now."

"Just for a few minutes, unfortunately. Ellie's grabbing some things then we'll be on our way back to the hospital."

"Robert told me about your son. I'm so sorry. Is he okay?"

"I think he will be. But what happened with Edward? Did he call?"

Sandy shook her head. "Not a word. Frankly I'm just as glad. He's been a real pain to work with lately." She glanced back at the counter, where Robert was taking an order. "I like him, though. Think you can hire Robert as a weeknight regular?"

Funny, I was just thinking that myself.

Margo sidestepped the question. "Is there anything you'd like me to do before I leave?"

"I don't think so." Sandy frowned. "Robert… we're okay, aren't we? We don't need anything?"

He glanced over the display case. "Maybe some more of those pecan-chocolate things."

"I've got plenty in the freezer."

As Margo headed toward the kitchen, Robert said, "I'll come with you." He followed her and closed the door behind them. "Margo?"

She turned and the sympathy in his eyes was almost her undoing.

"Are you okay?"

She compressed her lips so she wouldn't cry and nodded.

He didn't say anything else, just held out his arms, and for a minute she let him hold her. She closed her eyes and sank into the moment. Then, with a huge effort, she pulled herself back to reality.

Her little boy was lying in a hospital bed, waiting for her. "I have to get back…."

"Yes." He let her go, willingly. "I know."

"There's no way to thank you enough for all you've done. I could just throttle Edward for not showing up tonight of all nights." She glanced at the phone to see if the message light was flashing. It wasn't. "I don't suppose he called?"

"Not that we heard. But don't worry. I don't mind helping out. Sandy's a good kid. That's one employee you can count on, at least."

"Yes." Margo sighed. "I'm really sorry I screwed up your evening."

"I had no plans. And if I had, what was happening here was more important."

"Offering free food just doesn't seem enough anymore. Is there something I could do to help you? I know it isn't much money compared to what you're used to making, but could I pay you for your time, at least?"

He looked at her, clearly insulted.

"Forget I said that. I do understand that you did this as a favor." She swallowed. "One friend to another."

He tilted his head to one side and the intensity of his gaze increased. "A friend?"

She stared down at her feet. "This is all happening too fast."

He reached over and tucked a strand of hair behind her ear. Margo didn't want to think about what she must look like right now. With all her cold-water face rinses, she probably didn't have a trace of makeup left. And her hair was escaping from her clip, probably making her look even more harried than she felt.

"We have time. We can slow things down for a while if that's what you'd like. Certainly until you get Peter back home with you again." His hand dropped from her hair to her shoulder. His touch was light, but warm, and she wanted more of it.

Before Margo could respond to his suggestion, Ellie came dashing down the stairs with her stuffed backpack and Margo stepped away from him. "I have to go to the hospital—probably for the night."

"I'll be glad to lock up for you."

"Sandy knows the routine. If you could help her, that would be great."

Ellie was listening to their conversation with careful interest. Suddenly, she tugged on Margo's hand. "I'm hungry."

"I'm sorry, honey. Of course you are. Ask Sandy to make you a sandwich, okay?"

When Ellie had left the room, Margo focused on Robert again. "If you have someplace to go, I wouldn't mind if you and Sandy closed early."

"I have no place to go."

She let his words sink in, feeling implications that had probably not been intended. Or maybe they had. He took a step closer to her, and she was certain he was about to kiss her, but a clatter from the alley drove them apart.

Robert gave her a questioning look.

"I have no idea." She peeked out the back door cautiously. A small, mangy dog was tussling with one of their black garbage bags. He'd somehow managed to pull it out of the metal bin.

She glanced up and down the alley, but saw no one who might be the dog's owner. Meanwhile the dog kept chewing at his prize.

Robert stepped past her to the stoop. "Get out of there!"

The dog stopped what he was doing, sat pertly and gave them a heart-tugging look that said, "Sorry. I was just really, really hungry."

"Oh, you poor thing." His coat was dirty and matted and he wasn't wearing a collar. But his eyes were bright and intelligent-looking. Margo checked the alley again. "Where do you suppose he came from?"

"Good question." Robert stuffed the garbage back into the bag, then shut it tightly into one of the bins. All the while the dog just watched. When they moved back toward the door, he made a quiet crying sound.

Margo's heart melted. "We can't leave him out here."

"Want me to call animal control?"

She hesitated. She wanted to help, but what if the dog was dangerous? No way. Look at those eyes. Nevertheless, he could be carrying some sort of doggy disease. He didn't look very clean—still she decided to risk it. "Come here, boy."

He came. When he was within arm's length he sat and gave her that hopeful look again. Tentatively she reached out. His tail wagged eagerly as she scratched behind his ears.

"Careful," Robert said. "He could have fleas. Hang on while I check out front. Maybe he belongs to one of the customers."

Margo withdrew her hand, feeling even worse for the poor fellow than ever. She glanced back at the bistro, knowing Ellie waited inside, and Peter at the hospital would be wondering where she was, as well.

When Robert returned, he was shaking his head. "Tell you what. There's a doggy wash three blocks over. The owner negotiated a loan with the bank where I used to work. They supply big tubs, towels, even driers. Why don't I take the dog over there, then buy him some food?"

"That would be wonderful. Tomorrow we can put up signs in the neighborhood and try to find his owner."

"That leaves one problem. Where will he sleep tonight? Pets aren't allowed in my building."

"He could stay in my apartment," Margo said slowly. "That is, if you…?"

She and Robert exchanged one of those looks again. This time she was certain she was asking too much. But Robert just nodded. "I'll sleep on the couch and keep an eye on him."

She hesitated. "That doesn't sound very comfortable. You should feel free—"

He squeezed her arm. "I'll be fine. You should get going. Your son needs you."

ONCE ELLIE HAD SEEN her brother, and been reassured that he really was okay, Tom suggested that Catherine take her to their house.

"Why don't you go, too?" Margo said. "I'll spend the night with Peter, then you can return in the morning when we meet with the internist."

Tom hesitated. "Are you sure? I could stay with Peter, if you wanted to get back to your business."

Margo hated the fact that she was tempted to accept his offer. Early morning was when she baked the muffins and scones and prepared the daily soup. Not even Em could do those things for her, let alone the weekend staff. Peter would be sleeping most of the night, anyway….

But, no. She just couldn't leave him.

"I'll stay. You go home with Ellie and make sure she's fine."

Tom nodded. "Okay. That's the plan. We'll see you in the morning."

He gave her a hug, the first one since they'd separated, and Margo found it felt quite natural.

One year ago she'd been so angry at him, but now all she felt was relief. Living with Tom, trying to accommodate his demands, his need for a rigid schedule and a calm, quiet home, had exhausted and demoralized her.

True the divorce had exacted a price from all of them—including the kids. But she was herself again, and getting free from Tom had been necessary to make that happen.

"Call me if anything changes."

"I will." She gave Ellie a big hug and kiss. "Everything's going to be fine, honey. I'll talk to you tomorrow."

To Catherine, she merely nodded and offered a tight smile.

Peter did sleep quite well throughout the night, and so did Margo in the reclining chair next to his bed. In the morning the tests confirmed that they were dealing with diabetes.

Diabetes. It was real and it was happening to them.

"Okay. At least we know what the problem is." She gave Peter a reassuring smile and squeezed his hand.

"I want Daddy," he said quietly.

Trying not to feel as if her son had rejected her, Margo dialed Tom on the phone they'd requested last night.

"I'm getting in to the car now," he assured her.

"Daddy will be here soon," she told Peter, surprised to realize that she felt as relieved as her son by the news. Tom may not be a part of her life anymore, but it was a comfort to have someone she could depend upon where the children were concerned.

When Tom arrived, she filled him in quickly. "They're giving him an intravenous solution of electrolytes, water and insulin right now. In a little while we'll meet with the specialist, then a dietitian and psychologist."

"So, what will this mean exactly?" Tom betrayed his anxiety by smoothing the hair on the side of his head.

"The doctor I spoke to this morning thought that two injections of insulin each day should be all Peter will need for the first year. After that, they'll evaluate whether he might be a candidate for an insulin pump or multiple daily injections."

"Two shots." Tom's chest expanded on a deep breath. "I guess we'll have to learn how to do those."

Margo nodded.

"Catherine should really be here, too, then."

Margo wanted to protest, but she knew he was right. Undoubtedly, the task of checking Peter's blood sugar levels and injecting him with his insulin would often fall to Catherine. She had to be educated, just like they did.

While Tom dialed home, Margo returned to Peter's bedside. He'd eaten ravenously after the fasting test and now he was watching Saturday morning cartoons like any normal seven-year-old boy.

She decided to slip outside for some fresh air.

On her way she passed the hospital café, remembered she hadn't eaten anything all night, either, and ordered a coffee and a muffin.

Outside the bright spring sunshine felt like an affront. In Margo's current emotional state she would have preferred rain. Or at least fog.

She found a bench where she could sit, eat her breakfast and make a few calls. First she dialed the bistro and wasn't surprised when Robert answered.

"I've already taken the dog for a walk. He's upstairs sleeping in his new dog bed right now."

Dog bed. She made a note to settle up all the pet expenses with Robert when she got home. "Did the morning staff show up on time?"

"Yes. The only problem is that we're a little low

on muffins and scones. Plus, there doesn't seem to be any soup-of-the-day."

Her head spun with his efficiency. "If you check in the freezer, you'll find a tub of sunshine carrot soup and also dough for blueberry and bran muffins."

Robert listened as she explained how to thaw the soup and bake the muffins.

"I hate to saddle you with all this."

"Don't worry. Things are under control here. You need to keep your focus on your son."

He was right. But how could a single guy without children be so understanding?

Margo called Nora next. Her friend was full of sympathy when she heard about Peter's diagnosis. She was also supportive. "You can deal with this, Margo. It's going to be okay."

"Thank you. You don't know how much I needed to hear that right now."

With Robert and Nora's words buoying her, Margo left the sunshine to meet with her son's doctors.

ON SUNDAY AFTERNOON Peter was discharged from the hospital and Margo was both relieved and frightened. She desperately wanted life to return to normal, to have both her children back at home with her and to get operations at the bistro running smoothly again. All weekend long she'd been fielding calls from her employees about various problems. Robert had taken care of several. But she couldn't keep expecting him to help her this way.

Much as she wanted life to go back to the way it had been, Margo also had to accept that such a thing wasn't possible. Peter's diabetes was something the entire family had to learn to live with.

In the hospital the nurses had explained the importance of routine in managing Peter's disease. Treatment required a careful balance between his insulin injections, diet and exercise.

Because she loved cooking, Margo's children were used to homemade food, not frozen pizzas and packaged granola bars. The dietitian had complimented her on that. But she'd also warned that when Peter ate was almost as important as what he ate.

Tom had given her a dirty look then. One of his biggest complaints during their marriage was that meals were never ready when he wanted them to be ready.

But now she'd have to stick to a strict schedule. And the kids' habit of snacking on muffins or cookies between meals was something else they'd need to change.

Could she do this? Despite the pamphlets and

notes she'd stuffed into Peter's duffel bag, Margo was a little intimidated. The consequences of failure were huge. If the level of insulin in Peter's blood rose too high, he could fall into a coma. Conversely, if the levels were too low, he'd end up back where he started from…and she sure didn't want that.

After Peter was finally discharged, Margo took him out to her car. As she buckled him into the backseat, the silver of his new Medic Alert bracelet sparkled at her, reminding her of all the risks her little boy faced.

"Ready to go get your sister?" she asked him.

He nodded. Though it had only been a few days, he missed Ellie. She'd been staying at Tom's house all weekend, and Margo had missed her, too.

Right after their wedding Tom and Catherine had moved into a new house in Pacific Heights. Margo followed the instructions Catherine had thought-fully printed out, along with a hand-drawn map.

Since their consultations with the specialists on Saturday morning, Catherine hadn't returned to the hospital. She'd spent her weekend with Ellie, leaving Tom free to devote his time, like Margo, to Peter.

Now as she wound her way through the quiet streets with their grandiose homes, Margo tried to prepare herself for what she was about to see. It was difficult not to contrast this elegant, ritzy neighborhood with her own. SOMA had personality and culture, a hodgepodge of art galleries and warehouses, trendy hotels and small businesses. It teemed with life and people, dog lovers and young executives. Margo found it a fascinating place to live.

But she suspected the kids would probably prefer this neighborhood.

She pulled to a stop in front of a restored Victorian, one of the least ostentatious houses on the block. Black urns overflowing with ivy and geraniums sat on either side of the double front door. It felt bizarre to her when Peter raced up the walkway ahead of her and opened the door without knocking. Before she could say anything, he'd disappeared into the next room calling out, "Catherine. Dad. I'm home!"

The words jolted her like nothing else ever had. Home.

To her son and daughter this place—so strange to her—was as much a home as the apartment they shared with her.

And it was wonderful. No welcoming touch had been omitted—from the fresh flowers in a vase on a side table, to the brass umbrella stand and coatrack, to the charming rug in the middle of the hall.

The house even smelled like home. Could that be the scent of *freshly baking bread* in the air? If Catherine was a good cook, too, then she had absolutely nothing on the other woman. No wonder Tom looked so happy these days.

"Mom! I've been waiting for you." Ellie came running from the room that had swallowed Peter. She was wearing clothes that Margo didn't recognize. Apparently she and Catherine had gone on another shopping trip.

A moment later, Catherine and Tom made an entrance, with Peter between them. Catherine had something wrapped in a tea towel in her hands. "I know you've spent the entire weekend in the hospital, so I thought a tray of fresh buns might come in handy."

"Thank you." As Margo accepted the gift she suddenly felt light-headed. Maybe it was the crazy weekend, not much sleep, too much worry. Or maybe it was stepping into a Norman Rockwell painting, only to discover you didn't belong.

Just erase me from the picture and it would be perfect....

No. She couldn't let herself feel this way. Her apartment might not make a great Christmas card cover, but it was the kids' home, too.

"Come on, guys." She put an arm around each

of her children. "I think it's time for this crazy weekend to end."

"But you promised me a surprise." It wasn't like Peter to pout, but he was doing so now. "And I never got one."

Margo's stomach dipped as she realized she'd forgotten her promise. Then a sudden thought occurred to her. "Actually, you did. He's waiting for you at home right now." She squeezed Ellie's shoulder. "Waiting for *both* of you."

"What?" The kids gave her curious stares.

"It's a dog. We're babysitting him for a few days."

"A dog?" Peter looked at her with Christmas-morning-sized eyes. "Wow."

"Is this a joke?" Ellie wanted to know.

"I hope so," Tom muttered.

Margo ignored him. "No joke. We can't keep him forever, but for now he's all ours."

"Wow, a real dog, Mom? Not a stuffed one?"

Margo laughed. "Oh, he's real all right. Just wait until you see how much he eats."

As she ushered her children out to the car, Tom followed with Ellie's duffel bag. "I hope this pet thing really is temporary. You already have a lot on your plate."

And, obviously, he didn't think she could handle it. Despite her own reservations, Margo tightened her jaw stubbornly. "We'll be fine, Tom." But even as she drove away, she could see him standing on the sidewalk watching after her, shaking his head.

CHAPTER ELEVEN

Days Unemployed: 15

ON MONDAY Robert had two job interviews. Both seemed to go well. So well that he didn't have time to drop by Margo's for his usual soup and scone. He considered phoning and asking if he could come around later that evening.

But he had a feeling she would be overwhelmed and not welcome the interruption. This was Peter's first day at school since his diagnosis. Margo had planned a meeting with the teacher and the school vice principal.

Then there was the dog. So far, no one had claimed him. Robert didn't know if Margo meant to keep him. But her kids had been so excited to come home to the new pet that he knew the pressure to do so would be overwhelming. In some ways the stray dog had been the perfect distraction after their tough weekend.

But Robert had his misgivings about the situation. The dog was a nice animal with a sweet temperament. But Margo's apartment was tight on space and she didn't have a backyard. He wasn't sure a dog was the most sensible pet for her to own. For sure it was going to mean a lot of extra work and extra expense, as well.

And Robert didn't think Margo had either time or money to spare.

On Tuesday Robert had a meeting with his headhunter, then lunch with a fellow UCLA grad—a contact he hoped would provide a lead for a new position. Unfortunately the lead was a dead end and the lunch wasn't that great, either.

Besides, Robert missed Margo's soups. He missed Margo, period. It was strange how quickly he'd grown used to having her in his life. Two weeks ago he hadn't known Margo Evans existed. Now he couldn't get through an hour without thinking of her.

Though she'd thanked him over and over for his help this past weekend, to him it was no big deal. Taking care of the dog, lending a hand at the bistro—he'd been glad to do both of those things.

As for sleeping in Margo's apartment… He'd found that oddly endearing. Though he hadn't snooped in drawers or anything crazy like that, he'd felt closer to Margo when he was at her place.

On Wednesday he had a couple more interviews. The last one didn't end until five but as soon as he was free Robert grabbed the cable car from Montgomery Street to the turnaround point on Davis Street. He walked the rest of the way to Justin Herman Plaza, hoping to grab a quick bite.

Though he'd only lived here a year, he felt at home in this city and wasn't sorry he'd moved here, even if his relationship with Belinda hadn't worked out. From a career perspective, relocating to San Francisco certainly made sense. The city had a proud banking history—the mighty Wells Fargo Bank had its origins in this city and Montgomery Street was considered the Wall Street of the West.

He could go far in San Francisco.

As soon as he landed a job.

Robert walked restlessly along the broad expanse of concrete. He stopped to consider the mangled form of the Vaillancourt Fountain. Like a geyser, it shot out a spray of thousands of gallons of water at regular intervals. Standing well back from the wet zone, Robert watched the old fountain perform, then continued on his way.

His way to where?

He had no idea. All of a sudden none of the food on offer in the area had any appeal to him. He wanted soup. He wanted to see Margo.

He took a cab to SOMA and arrived shortly

after six. For a change, Sandy and Edward were both on the job. Sandy served him the soup of the day and slipped him an extra scone.

"Are you sure you don't want to work here?" She rolled her eyes in Edward's direction. "I sure do miss having you around."

"Sorry. I love Margo's soups but not enough to make my career in the food services industry. Speaking of Margo…" He checked around the restaurant to no avail. "Is she here?"

"I think—" Sandy's response was cut off when the dog from the alley came bounding out of the kitchen. Margo followed, pink-cheeked and holding an empty collar and leash.

"His head just slipped out like his fur had been oiled or something."

Robert stepped in front of the dog and held out his hand. "Here, boy. Remember me?"

The stray stopped short, ears perked, tail wagging. Yeah, he remembered him all right. Robert scratched the side of the dog's neck, then patted his side.

"Oh, great. Don't let Boy go," Margo said.

"Boy?"

"That's what we've been calling him. We still haven't managed to pick a name. Everyone wants something different."

"Boy works for me. Pass me the collar." He

held out his hand and, after a pause, she passed it over. Robert snapped open the clasp, then slipped the leather strap around Boy's neck. The dog reacted immediately to the unwelcome restraint, practically pulling Robert out to the street. "He's raring to go."

"Maybe so, but we only have time for a quick bathroom break. The kids are upstairs working on homework." She fell silent, then said, more slowly, "I haven't seen you for a while."

Robert stopped and widened his stance against the dog's straining. "I've had a bunch of job interviews."

"Oh. Well, that's good."

"Yeah. Hopefully I'll get a nibble or two."

She held out her hand and for a minute he stared at it, before he realized she wanted the leash. He passed it to her, electricity crackling at the smooth brush of her skin against his.

The dog was small, but he was strong. As soon as he sensed Margo on the other end of the lead, he started to strain again. Margo rolled her eyes. "He doesn't seem to be trained to wear one of these."

"Obedience school might be a good idea."

"If I only had the time to take him. Maybe I should have turned him over to the SPCA, after all.

He's way more work than I thought. On the other hand, Peter and Ellie love him to bits."

But they were too young to do any of the work associated with looking after a dog in an apartment in the city. Neither one had the strength to take him out for a walk, that was for sure.

"Well…" Robert was about to ask if he could walk the dog for her, when he realized what day it was. "Aren't the kids supposed to be with their dad on Wednesdays?"

"Yes, but Tom had business in L.A. today and he wasn't sure what time his flight…" Her words trailed off and her expression grew anxious. "Speaking of the devil…"

Robert followed her gaze to a silver Mercedes pulling into a parking space near the bistro. He recognized Margo's ex-husband as he climbed out of the driver's seat. The frown lines on Tom's brow deepened as he looked from Margo, to the dog, then to Robert.

"Where are the kids?"

Margo swallowed, then raised her chin. "Hi to you, too, Tom. You remember Robert?"

Tom's appraisal was brief and dismissive. "From the wedding, yes." He looked at Boy next. "So this is the new dog. Not very well-trained, is he?"

As Tom spoke, Boy lifted his leg and peed on a wrought-iron grill protecting a graceful oak tree.

"Not yet, he isn't. The kids are inside doing their schoolwork. Did you want to go up and say hi to them?"

"That depends." Tom checked his watch. "I take it they've eaten their dinner?"

Margo's jaw tightened. "We were just about—"

"Margo. Regular meals are important."

"I know. I'm just running a tiny bit late. The dog hasn't been out since noon and I wasn't expecting the kids to be home tonight, at all, until Catherine called a few hours ago."

"God, Margo. Why does putting a meal on the table have to be such a big deal to you? If you'd just—"

Robert started backing away. This was turning into a squabble and he figured he'd better butt out, before he said something rash. Tom was being a jerk and he longed to jump in on Margo's behalf. Yeah, regular meals were important for a diabetic. But would a half hour really make a difference? He didn't think so.

But before Robert could complete his escape, the kids came rushing out the door.

"I thought that was your car," Ellie said as she raced into her father's arms. Robert's animosity toward the man softened as he saw Tom's smile.

"Hi, sweetheart. Hi, son." He reached an easy arm around the little boy's shoulders. "How was school today?"

Robert glanced at Margo. She'd managed to pull Boy in tightly next to her and she was watching her ex interacting with the children, smiling ruefully. She caught his gaze and cocked her eyebrows as if to say, *He isn't all bad.*

And he wasn't, Robert realized, with a rush of relief. Tom was actually a pretty decent father. His kids obviously loved him and felt a close connection to him.

Unlike Andrew, they didn't need a father figure in their lives. Maybe he'd been worried about Margo's kids more than he'd needed to.

When Tom and the kids decided to walk down the block for a burger, he waited a few seconds then asked, "Boy obviously would appreciate a longer walk. How about you?"

Margo passed him the lead. "Absolutely."

MARGO AND ROBERT ENDED up walking the dog for over an hour. When they got back to the bistro, she looked at her watch and almost shrieked.

"Oh, my lord. My friends are going to be here in less than an hour. And I still have to bake a fruit crisp."

"Can I help?" Robert pulled her in close enough

to give her a kiss. But now that Boy had seen home, he was tugging on his leash again and standing still was virtually impossible.

"You'd better not come in," Margo decided reluctantly. "Tonight you'd be more of a distraction than a help."

"And you don't want to be distracted?"

Actually she did. That was the problem. Robert ran a hand down her arm and she shivered.

"Maybe I should come by later? After your friends have gone?"

"That would be nice."

He left then, not a moment too soon, as she'd been about to weaken and invite him inside. Instead she took Boy around to the back entrance, settled him upstairs in the apartment, then went to the kitchen to make her crisp. Earlier Margo had invited an old high school friend of hers, Rosie DeWitt, to join the girls for coffee.

She and Rosie had reconnected a year ago at their high school reunion. They'd promised to keep in touch, but Margo had just been going through her divorce then and she'd forgotten about the commitment. Last week, though, when Selena had called them the Singles With Kids group, she'd thought of Rosie.

Rosie also had a young son and worked full-time as a political aide. The boy's father wasn't in the picture, so Rosie knew all about juggling work and family commitments. Margo had dug up her number and given her a call.

"We aren't a formal support group or anything. Just friends who like to talk about our kids and our jobs and well…life."

"I'd love to join you for coffee," Rosie had said quickly. "The men I work with don't get kids, at all."

As it turned out Rosie was the first to arrive that evening. She bounced in still dressed in her business suit from work, her long curly black hair pulled back in a ponytail. "Hey, Margo, great place."

"Thanks." Margo usually felt proud when someone complimented her bistro. But tonight all she could think about were her unpaid bills and the upcoming meeting with her loan manager.

She'd dropped the cash flow statement off yesterday and had managed to put off a face-to-face meeting with a loan officer until next week. Her stomach hurt just to think about it.

To distract herself, she offered Rosie something to drink. She cleaned the frothing arm of the La Marzocco. "What kind of coffee would you like?"

Rosie rattled off her request without pausing to think. "Non-fat, white chocolate mocha with a shot of espresso and whipped cream."

Margo grinned to herself and reached for the bottle of skim milk. "Coming right up. The others will be here shortly."

"Great." Rosie perched on one of the stools and leaned over the counter. "So how have you been? You were still kind of shell-shocked over the divorce last time I saw you. But you're looking good now."

"Thanks. It's been a busy year. Tom is remarried for one thing."

"And…? How are you doing with that?"

"Fine. Sort of. Oh, I don't mind about Tom having found someone new. It's getting used to the kids having a stepmother in their lives that's taking some adjustment."

Margo filled Rosie in on the other news in her life. The diabetes. The stray dog.

"Wow. Sounds like you've had quite the week."

Nora and Selena strolled in together then. Everyone introduced themselves, and Margo handed Rosie her mocha, then started Selena's espresso and Nora's chai latte. Once the drinks were ready, they retired to the annex, where Margo curled up on the couch, more than ready to relax and have a good chat.

"So how old is your son, Rosie?" Nora wanted to know. "My Danny is six."

"Casey's only four. I can't believe how much

he's changed this last year. He's definitely a little boy now, not a toddler, you know?"

"I remember when Drew was that age. When we'd go for walks, he'd point out every truck on the road. And we had to stop to pet every dog…." Selena turned to Margo. "Speaking of which, I hear you've adopted one."

"Sort of. I'm not sure if it's permanent. He's so cute and good-natured, I'm sure someone will claim him before too long."

"Well, if they don't and if you decide he's too much work for you, let me know. I've been thinking now that Drew's older it might be good for him to have the responsibility of looking after a pet." Selena took a sip of her espresso. She was wearing another great piece of turquoise jewelry today— a ring that kept catching Margo's eye.

"I'll keep your offer in mind, but be warned. The dog is sweet, but he doesn't respond to any command except 'come.' And he sure does have a lot of energy. The other day he destroyed an entire package of Ellie's washable markers."

"Anyone ready for dessert?" Nora asked.

"Thanks, Nora," Rosie said as she was handed a dish of the crisp. She took a small taste. "Wow, Margo. This is exceptional."

"Thanks." Margo smiled at Rosie's rapturous expression as she dug in to her dessert.

"Maybe you should talk Tom and his new wife into taking the dog," Nora said. "Didn't you say their new house is in Pacific Heights?"

Rosie sat up tall. "Is that right? Impressive." Like any true San Franciscan, Rosie knew what it meant to live in a neighborhood like Pacific Heights. "Obviously your ex is doing well for himself."

"Their home is perfect. So much nicer and bigger than mine."

"A house is just a material possession," Nora reminded her. "Love is what your children really need. Never forget that."

"You're so right about that. But lately life has been such a struggle. On top of everything, I've had some issues with the bank lately."

"Nothing serious, I hope?" Rosie's keen eyes flashed with concern.

"Not really." Margo couldn't admit how precarious her financial situation was. During their walk Robert had reiterated his promise to help her find efficiencies that would improve her bottom line. She appreciated his offer, but couldn't help worrying it would be too little, too late. The produce bill had come in today and she was going to have to dip into her savings to cover it.

"Hey, Margo." Nora tapped her shoulder. "Isn't that your guy?"

Margo craned her neck to see, then caught her breath. Robert had returned as promised. He was a little early, but she didn't mind, at all.

CHAPTER TWELVE

"IS THAT ROBERT?" Selena glanced over her shoulder, then drew in her breath sharply. "Oh, yum. It is, isn't it?"

"You didn't say anything about a new guy in your life." Rosie gave her a jab. "And he's so cute...."

"Would you all please stop staring at him?" Margo focused on her coffee cup. "I feel like I'm in high school, again."

"Only with better skin," Nora said.

"And bigger boobs."

"Rosie!" Margo knew her cheeks had to be bright pink by now.

"Don't worry, Margo. We aren't going to embarrass you anymore." Selena downed her last swallow of espresso. "Come on, ladies. Let's clear out of here."

"But it's still early."

"I'm with Selena," Nora said. "I think you and

Robert need some alone time. We'll talk later, okay? Call me."

Before Margo knew it, all her friends were gone, leaving her alone in the annex room. But not for long.

Robert cleared his throat. He was still standing by the French doors, which the women had left open. "I didn't mean to close down the party early."

"That's okay." Nora was right. They did need some alone time. She moved to make room for him to join her on the sofa and when he did, brushing his thigh against hers, warmth infused every cell in her body.

The burning intensified when she saw how he was looking at her. His obvious desire filled her with the crazy heat she'd experienced when he kissed her. For a few moments she remembered what it was like to be young and in love.

But she wasn't young anymore. She was thirty-four years old. The mother of two children. A responsible business owner. How could she be falling so crazily in love with a man she'd known for less than a month?

"Where are Ellie and Peter?"

"Decided to go home with their father." She dropped her gaze, so he couldn't tell she was thinking about the empty apartment and the potential for privacy that it offered. It was way too soon for *that* to be happening here.

She had to cool things. And quickly.

"So tell me more about the job interviews you had today."

He gave her a look that told her he knew exactly what she was trying to do by changing the subject. Still, he went along with it. "They were both assistant general manager positions." He gave her an outline of the job requirements.

Margo noticed his passion and smiled. "Have you always known banking is what you want to do?"

"Oh, yeah. It runs in the family. Mom was in the business, too. She passed away a few years ago. What about your parents? Do they live around here?"

"Retired in Florida."

"Any siblings?"

"None. I hated that."

"Me, too. Is that why you had two kids?"

"I would have had more, but Tom was against it."

"More, huh?" Robert's gaze lingered on her and she sensed a question in them.

She was almost afraid to ask. But she couldn't resist. "Do you want to have kids?"

He nodded.

"Oh."

"You sound surprised."

"Well, there were a few times when you gave me the impression that you don't like children very much."

He looked away from her, and Margo's heart dropped. She'd been right. This was going to be an issue. She started to get out of her chair. "If you have problems with my kids, there's no point in us—"

Robert reached for her hand. "Wait. I did have concerns about your children at first. Can I tell you why?"

Reluctantly, she sank back into her seat, not at all sure she was interested in his so-called explanation.

"The fiancée I told you about? Belinda?"

"Yes…?"

"She has a son. His name is Andrew. He still calls me sometimes. He was really upset when I didn't go to his birthday party a few weeks ago."

"Why didn't you go?"

"Belinda has asked me not to see him anymore. She wants him bonding with her new boyfriend. I see her point, but it hasn't been easy. Strange as it may sound I miss that kid. And I know he feels like I abandoned him."

"Oh, Robert." She put her hand over his, feeling

his hurt and his sense of responsibility. Warmth rushed over her for this man who would care so much about disappointing a child.

"When love goes wrong, it's one thing to deal with it as an adult. Quite another when children are in the picture."

And that was why he had hesitated to get involved with her. "What changed your mind with me?"

"Frankly, I just couldn't stay away."

Her heart raced.

"But tonight, when I saw your kids with their father, I realized that your kids already have a dad in their lives. Andrew didn't."

Robert turned his hand so he could hold on to hers. He intertwined their fingers, then pulled her closer so he could kiss her.

Their lips touched softly, their mouths opened perfectly to each other. "Oh." Margo sighed.

"I love kissing you."

She knew what he meant. She felt exactly the same way. The connection was deeper than just physical, which ought to be great, only was it? This didn't feel at all like the casual, fun relationship Nora had suggested she needed.

It felt like falling in love. Something she definitely didn't have room for in her life right now.

FRIDAY MORNING the kids were up brushing their teeth before Margo realized it was a professional development day for their teachers. She stared at the notation on the calendar, wondering how she'd missed it.

She went to the bathroom door. "Did you guys know you don't have school today?"

They nodded, unable to talk with toothbrushes in their mouths.

Other kids might have taken the chance to sleep in. But her two were early risers, like her.

"I'm going downstairs to put some muffins into the oven. I'll bring some up for breakfast when they're ready."

Peter spat. "Will you bring one for Boy?"

The dog was in the bathroom with them, sitting on the tile floor, wagging his tail. He looked darn happy and well he should. Margo had already taken him outside for his morning constitutional. It would be so much easier if she could only open a door and let him out to a backyard to do his business.

"No. Boy shouldn't eat people food. You can give him two scoops of the stuff under the kitchen sink."

She ran downstairs and removed the bowl of muffin batter from the fridge, then put spoonfuls into the tray she'd prepared last night. Em popped in briefly to grab a bag of bagels for the front.

"Busy morning," she said.

"I'll be right out there to help you," Margo promised. She popped the muffins into the oven, washed her hands, then joined Em. She should have felt great, seeing customers lined practically to the door, but all she could think of was something Robert had told her the other day.

"You're actually losing money on your breakfast crowd, Margo," he'd said. "You've got to adjust your prices."

But which items and by how much? She couldn't go too high or her customers would take their business elsewhere. Robert was working on the numbers and hoped to have something for her in time for the meeting with the bank next week. But she was still worried that the changes wouldn't happen in time to make a difference.

"One skinny decaf and a berry bran muffin." Margo rang in the sale, then used tongs to place the muffin into a parchment bag. She handed it to the young businesswoman, then smiled at the next person in line. She'd helped half a dozen customers before the buzzer sounded on her watch.

"Sorry, Em. I've got to get those muffins out of the oven."

She left the poor woman with a lineup only

marginally shorter than it had been fifteen minutes ago. In the kitchen, she pulled the muffins from the oven just in time, then took a tray upstairs for the kids.

She served yogurt with the muffins and slices of oranges. When Ellie and Peter were finished eating, she tested Peter's blood then gave him his insulin. Even with both arms around Boy's neck, he still winced whenever he had to get a shot. And she still felt like the worst parent in the world giving it to him.

"Thanks, Peter. All done." She noticed Ellie clipping the leash on to Boy.

"Can we take him for a walk, Mom?"

"Sweetheart, no. Maybe when you're older and he's had some obedience training. Why don't you guys watch a movie?"

She didn't like leaving them sitting in front of the television while she went back to work, but she didn't have a choice. The bistro was always extra busy right through lunchtime and one person couldn't handle that on their own.

"Sorry, Em," she apologized, when she finally joined her behind the counter. "I forgot the kids didn't have school today, or I would have brought in extra help."

"That's okay," Em said, but clearly she'd been struggling on her own. The container for used coffee grounds was overflowing, all the counters were sticky and dirty dishes littered the sink. Em, who always cleaned up behind herself, had obviously been run off her feet.

Even with two working, there was barely time to grab a drink of water, or go to the washroom. Every now and then, Margo dashed upstairs to check on the kids. When the first movie ended, she started another.

"I'm bored." Peter stared out the window at the sunshine. Margo knew the kids would love to be out on their bikes, or with friends at the playground.

"We'll do something fun tonight," she promised. "But right now I have to go back to work."

She gave them sandwiches and apple slices for lunch, then ran downstairs. The midday crowd was steady—Margo barely had time to lift her head from the cash register and order pad. So she was startled when around one o'clock a familiar voice asked for an iced latte. Margo did a double take. "Catherine?"

Tom's wife was dressed casually in jeans and a blue-and-white striped shirt. Her sunglasses rested on the top of her head and her chestnut hair gleamed as if it had been freshly brushed, then sprayed into its perfect position.

She looked relaxed and casual, yet poised. And

Margo was instantly aware of how disheveled she must appear in comparison. She smoothed a stray curl behind her ear. "This is a surprise."

"You didn't know Peter called me?"

Margo shook her head as Em handed Catherine the icy drink she'd ordered. Catherine slid three dollars across the counter and Margo automatically opened the till and stacked the bills in the appropriate tray.

"I'm sorry. I suppose I should have insisted on speaking to you, but Peter told me you were busy."

"I was."

"Yes. I see." Catherine tried another smile. "According to Peter, he and Ellie don't have school today."

"That's true."

"And it's so lovely outside, I was wondering if I could maybe take them out for a few hours."

Margo should have seen it coming, but she hadn't. It took a few seconds for her to find her voice. "That's very nice of you. I'm sure the kids would love that. Just a minute and I'll run and get them." She turned to Em, who was frothing milk for the next order. "I won't be long."

"It's no problem."

"You're a saint, Em." As Margo dashed up the stairs for about the tenth time that day, she prayed that Em would never quit. She'd be lost without her. If her financial situation ever improved, the first thing she would do was give the woman a well-deserved raise.

In the apartment Margo found both kids sitting on the couch, looking like zombies. Feeling more guilty than ever, Margo switched off the television. "Okay kids, change of plans."

"Did Catherine come?" Peter's face brightened.

Margo nodded. He sounded so excited, she didn't have the heart to chastise him for calling his stepmother without asking her first. "Put on your shoes and a hoodie. It's not as warm outside as it looks."

When they were ready, she rubbed sunscreen on their cheeks then brought them down to Catherine.

"I'll have them home before dinner," Catherine promised. As they headed for the door, she reminded the kids to say goodbye to their mother. Only then did Ellie and Peter run back to give her a kiss.

Margo tore her gaze from the door.

"You're doing the best you can," Em said quietly. "Don't feel guilty."

"Thanks, Em." She made a production of checking the display unit. "Wow, we sure sold a lot of cookies today. I'd better get some more."

She escaped to the kitchen just in time. As the tears came, she gave herself a few moments to feel sorry for herself. It didn't help that she had only herself to blame. If she'd been better organized, she would have made sure she was free today. Then *she* would be taking the kids to the park right now, not Catherine.

Not that she had the money right now to hire extra staff….

Margo rested her head against the cool stainless steel refrigerator. Was Em right? Was she just being hard on herself? When she'd worked in the law firm, she'd never had trouble managing her workload. But she'd had a personal assistant at the office and a full-time nanny at home.

Still, other single mothers managed to juggle looking after children as well as their jobs. Selena, Rosie and Nora all did. Why couldn't she?

CHAPTER THIRTEEN

Days Unemployed: 19

ROBERT WAS EXPECTING to hear back from his previous days' interviews before noon. When eleven-thirty rolled around and he still hadn't received a call on his BlackBerry, he decided to go for a walk.

Out of habit he ended up in the financial district. He strolled by his old office tower and watched his former coworkers spill out of the building for their requisite thirty-minute lunch break. They were entitled to more time than that, but almost none of them took it, unless they were on a business luncheon with a client.

After that, he hopped a cable car to Belinda's apartment. Her kitchen window faced the street. The drapes were partially drawn so all Robert could see was the toaster that sat on the breakfast table. He remembered how no matter how much he'd fiddled with the settings, the toast had come out either too light or too dark.

Next to the kitchen window was the balcony off the eating nook. A new bike was chained to the railing. It was the exact model he'd picked out of the store front window. Had Belinda bought it for him? Or the new guy?

Robert wondered how Andrew was doing. He hadn't received any calls since Belinda had laid down the law. Hopefully that meant everything was okay.

Robert checked the time. Three o'clock. He pulled out his BlackBerry for the umpteenth time. No missed calls. He sighed, feeling the disappointment like an extra five pounds between his shoulder blades.

He decided to catch the next cable car. He rode it to the end of the line, then kept moving on foot. Soon he stood in front of another window.

Margo's Bistro. The soup of the day was Red-and-White Surprise. He inhaled the heady aroma of wonderful, home-cooked food, then pushed on the door. Em was working at the counter alone. He lined up behind a guy with baggy pants and dread-locks. When it was his turn, he ordered the soup.

"Interesting name," he said. "What is it?"

"Red pepper and leek." Em sounded as if she'd explained this many times already that day. "It's actually delicious, believe it or not."

"I believe it." He had faith in anything Margo

made, with the possible exception of muffins. He watched as Em ladled first a red soup, then a white soup into a wide, shallow bowl. Both were quite thick and stayed on their respective sides of the bowl. Then Em took a knife and ran a line through the center, blending the two colors in a zigzag pattern.

"Would you like a—"

"Herbed scone, please." He paid for the food, then went to his usual table. Though the door was closed, he could tell someone was in the kitchen. Margo, he hoped. He planned to go and talk to her, but first he finished the soup, which was amazing, full of flavor with a smooth, but substantial, texture.

When he'd scraped out the last spoonful, he headed for the kitchen as if he had every right to push past the door marked Employees Only. As he'd guessed, Margo was there, stirring something on the stove. She was wearing her apron and her hair had been pinned up the way she usually wore it when she was at work.

The edgy feeling that had nagged him all day disappeared at the sight of her.

"I had a crappy day. Until now, that is. How about you?" He moved closer, tempted by the white skin at the nape of her neck. He wished he had the right to put his hand there. To turn her toward him.

But she continued stirring whatever it was she was cooking on the stove. Without even glancing in his direction she said, "I bet my crap beats your crap."

He could tell she was serious. "What happened?"

She told him about the kids having the day off from school and how unprepared she'd been and how Tom's wife had been the one to step forward and save the day.

"The kids just came home from spending three hours at the park. They were flying kites. For all that time." She shook her head as if she couldn't believe it. "I've never been able to get a kite to stay up for more than five minutes."

"It's not that difficult. I could teach you."

She shook her head and tucked her chin lower, still not looking at him. He wasn't Dr. Phil or anything, but he had a feeling her kite-flying ability wasn't the real issue here.

"You're a good mother."

She flicked off the gas range and finally faced him. Her red-tinged eyes gleamed with tears. "Once, I thought I was, but lately I'm not so sure. Opening this bistro was my dream…but what if I've taken on way too much? I don't have time to make a success of this place and raise two small children as well. Even the time I do find to spend with Ellie and Peter, I'm never really focusing on them. I'm always wondering if my staff is doing a proper job or if they're going to run out of soup or scones or cookies."

He thought about that. "When you were working for that law firm, you must have put in long hours, too."

"At least I pulled in a good paycheck for my efforts. I could afford a nanny to do the cleaning and laundry and the million other jobs that pile up around a house. I hadn't realized until you went over my books how much money I've been losing."

"Information is a good thing. You'll be able to turn this place around." He felt guilty that he'd spent his morning wandering aimlessly instead of coming up with recommendations that would help her. "I have nothing planned for tomorrow. I'll spend the whole day going over your records. I'm sure we can come up with something. In the meantime, let's fix your crappy day. Where are the kids?"

"Upstairs, playing. They aren't very happy about it, though. They want to be outside, but according to Tom, my neighborhood isn't safe enough for that." She leaned against the counter.

"This upcoming weekend is one they're supposed to spend with me, but they've both hinted rather broadly that they'd rather have gone home with Catherine."

It sounded like distraction techniques were in order. For Margo and her kids. "Your evening staff will be here in an hour. Do you think you could skip out for a bit?"

"I don't know. Em's already done a lot of covering for me lately."

"It's not that busy." Em spoke from the doorway. She eyed the two of them, then went to a cupboard and pulled out a bag of bagels. "Take off early for a change, Margo. Things will be fine here."

"But—"

Em stopped her with a look. "I mean it, Margo. Take a break. You need it and your kids need it."

When the other woman had left the room, Margo hesitated a minute, then pulled off her apron and stuffed it in the hamper. She turned to Robert. "Looks like I have some free time. Now what do I do with it?"

"Play."

She laughed. "Sounds like fun. But what?"

"Do your kids like soccer?"

"I don't think they've ever tried it."

"I thought all kids played soccer these days."

He'd loved the sport when he was little. His mom had enrolled him in the neighborhood league every year.

"Tom was never interested in putting the kids into competitive sports."

"Every kid ought to learn to play soccer. Come on, call them down and let's go to the park."

"But we don't own a soccer ball."

"I do."

"*You* do?"

He could read the question in her voice. It had to do with more than soccer. Up until now, he hadn't had much interaction with her kids. Truth was, even though Ellie and Peter seemed to have a good relationship with their dad, he was still a little nervous about getting too close to them.

But he couldn't stand seeing Margo so unhappy. He had to do something to help her. "I'll go home and get the ball. How about we meet in the school playground in fifteen minutes?"

THE KIDS AND MARGO were waiting by the time Robert pulled into the vacant teachers' lot. Margo had tied the dog to a nearby tree, and Boy looked as eager as Peter and Ellie when Robert pulled the soccer ball and some orange pylons from the trunk.

"What are those for?" Peter wanted to know.

"We can use them to play some warm-up games. Then later, they'll be our goal posts." Robert showed the kids how to kick the ball with the side of their foot, then he set up the pylons so they could practice ball control.

Peter was still young and didn't have much coordination, but both Margo and Ellie were surprisingly good. Robert ran through a few simple drills to teach them the basics, then suggested they split into boys against girls for a little match.

Soon all four of them were running and laughing and vying for a chance to kick the ball. When a young father showed up at the park with his daughter and asked if they could join in, both Ellie and Peter shouted, "Sure!"

They were friendly, happy kids, who seemed delighted to be out in the late afternoon sunshine. Even Margo had no trouble cutting loose and chasing after the ball, every bit as determined as Ellie and Peter to be the one to get to it first.

Robert loped around the field, feeding the ball back to the kids every chance he got and making the occasional run at the goal to get everyone excited.

The other father was pretty skilled at the game and a few times they tussled over the ball, with the kids cheering in the background.

About forty minutes after they'd started playing, Margo held up her hand to stop a play. "Peter, are you all right?"

"I feel a little spinny."

"Do you mean dizzy?" Margo went to her son and tilted his face up so she could see him. "We should go home."

"But I'm having fun."

"Well, I have a juice box in my purse. Maybe if you sat down for a minute and drank that, you'd be able to play a little more." The look she gave Robert was anxious. "At the hospital they warned us that if he was more active than usual his blood sugar could dip."

Robert nodded. "My buddy had to watch out for the same thing."

The other father and daughter thanked them for the game, then made their way to the monkey bars at the other end of the schoolyard.

Robert kicked the ball to Ellie. "Want to practice shots while your brother has his drink?"

"Sure." Ellie followed him to one of the makeshift goal nets.

He took up goalie position and let her shoot from about fifteen feet away. "So, do you like soccer?"

"It's fun." She landed a big kick and sent the ball sailing over his shoulder.

"Good one." He ran for the ball, then tossed it

to her for another try. They played for several minutes, before Ellie seemed to get tired of the drill.

She tapped the ball a few times with her toe, then glanced at her mother and Peter. They were still sitting on the side of the field. Ellie tilted her head and looked at Robert thoughtfully. The quiet, dark-haired girl favored her father in both looks and deportment, as far as Robert could tell. But in that moment, in that careful, assessing glance she gave him, he could see a resemblance to her mother.

"Are you going to marry my mom?"

Robert didn't know how to answer Ellie's question.

"Your mom and I haven't known each other very long." That hadn't stopped them from enjoying several passionate kisses already, but it was still true.

Ellie tapped the soccer ball in his direction, then moved closer. "That's what Dad said about Catherine at first."

"Well, sometimes friends do end up getting married," Robert conceded. "But not always." He showcased some fancy footwork with the ball, hoping to distract her, but Ellie didn't even notice.

"So you *might* get married?"

Robert rubbed his hands on the front of his

sweatshirt. He glanced over at Margo. She was tossing the juice box into the trash. Any second she and Peter would be rejoining them.

Hurry, he urged them. *Get here before she says anything else.*

"It's okay if you do," Ellie went on to say. "Then I'd have two moms *and* two dads."

Robert saw the situation from her point of view. Poor kid was just trying to sort out her world. She'd seen her father remarry, so in her mind it was just a question of time before her mother did the same.

But her question still made him nervous. Was he making another big mistake here?

He glanced at Margo, felt the familiar warmth flood over him at just the sight of her. If he was, it was too late to stop what he'd started now.

ON SATURDAY, true to his word, Robert spent the day at Margo's going over the manual that had come with her computer accounting package and making lists of his ideas for improving profitability.

Meanwhile, Margo went out with the kids to buy a new calendar, a really big calendar with stickies to mark birthdays, doctor's appointments and, most importantly, no-school days. The kids helped her apply all the stickers to the appropriate days, and once that was done, she went through the school calendar and made sure she had every holiday, professional development day and parent-teacher interview day duly noted.

She tacked the calendar to the front hall closet, then pulled out the kids' school backpacks. If she wanted to make good on her resolution to be more organized in the future, this was where she had to start.

She dumped out the contents to the floor. Peter's pack was a mess of old cookie crumbs, scrunched-up spelling tests, rocks and sticks. She sorted out the garbage, saved the treasures, then checked the papers to see if there were any notes from the teacher.

She found an announcement for a gay pride and family diversity assembly on Monday, and another asking for parent volunteers for the annual sports day a month away. She signed up for the afternoon, then made a note on her calendar to hire extra help to work with Em on that day.

After she was done with Peter's backpack, she tackled Ellie's. This one was a breeze by comparison, as her daughter was a bit of a neat freak like her father. Margo found another notice about the family diversity assembly, but that was it.

Margo hung the packs on their pegs in the closet, then headed to the kitchen. Tom had been his usual pedantic self the other day, but he had made one valid point. It was more important than ever that the family eat regular, healthy meals. She planned out a menu for the entire week, then took the kids grocery shopping so they'd have everything they needed on hand.

At the end of the day Robert broke off from the accounting to help her make dinner, then later they played board games with the children.

It all felt so normal and natural, that Margo couldn't quite believe it. Robert left for home shortly after the kids went to bed, then on Sunday he came back just after lunch, to make good on his promise to take everyone to the park. After two hours of soccer Margo invited Robert home for dinner again.

"It's roast beef tonight," she told him.

"Then beef on a bun for school tomorrow," Ellie said.

"And shepherd's pie for Monday night," Peter added.

Robert blinked.

"Mommy raked leaves and now we're organized," Peter explained.

Ellie gave a world-weary sigh. "He means she turned over a new leaf. Not *raked* leaves, Peter."

"It's the same thing." Peter's face reddened. "Isn't it, Mommy?"

Margo was trying not to laugh. "Give or take a few leaves, yes, I suppose that's true."

"Anyway," Robert said, "I love roast beef and I love your mom's cooking so I'm definitely accepting that invitation."

The four of them plus Boy entered from the back alley, so they wouldn't need to troop through the bistro. Margo resisted the urge to check on the business. This was the first time since she'd opened that she'd taken an entire weekend off.

But she'd needed the break. And the kids had soaked up the extra attention. If something dire happened at the bistro, she was sure one of her staff would come and let her know.

After their energetic afternoon, Boy flopped onto his dog bed and went straight to sleep. Meanwhile, the kids were content to go to their rooms and finish homework for school the next day. Peter was supposed to read for a half hour, while Ellie had spelling words to memorize.

Robert followed Margo into the kitchen. It was much smaller and infinitely more basic than the one downstairs. Up here she had an electric stove and oven, a ten-year-old microwave and a dishwasher that sounded about as loud as a carwash.

She preheated the oven, then rubbed olive oil and a spice mixture into her roast.

"That smells good." Robert placed a bottle of

Australian Shiraz on the counter. Either he traveled with wine in his trunk, or he'd anticipated her dinner invitation. Margo wasn't going to complain, either way. She handed him the corkscrew.

A few minutes later they were both on the sofa with their wine. In the stillness, Margo was suddenly uncomfortable. "Would you like some cheese and crackers? I'll—"

"Don't get up." Robert took her hand and folded his fingers through hers.

"But I'm—"

"Margo." Robert took his time saying her name, making it sound like a love letter. "It's okay. We can sit here for a few minutes, can't we?"

"I should be—" She stopped. At any given time there were always a dozen jobs she could be doing. But maybe what was happening here, between her and Robert, deserved her attention right now.

She looked at him. His cheeks were still ruddy from the exercise and his hair had been whipped around by the wind. As for his eyes, they seemed more blue than ever. Maybe that was just because he had them focused so intently on her right now.

Warmth. Longing. She could feel his emotions, just as surely as she could taste the rich body of the wine against her tongue. If the kids weren't in the next room, she was pretty sure they'd be kissing right now. In fact, she was awfully tempted to take the risk anyway.

"It's been a great weekend."

Did he mean that? "All we did was hang out with my kids."

"I'm okay with that. Not that I would object to being alone with you for a while."

"We're alone right now."

His gaze dropped to her mouth. "I meant *really* alone."

He ran his fingers from her hand, up her arm then lightly touched her cheek.

Chemistry. Every cell in her body felt it.

"I want to kiss you, Margo."

She wanted the same thing. So badly. But as she darted a quick look at the kids' closed bedroom doors, she heard him sigh.

"It's not the right time or place. I know that. I just wanted to tell you how I was feeling." He touched the side of her face again with a feather-light gesture. "Maybe on Wednesday…?"

"Yes." On Wednesday the kids would be with Tom and Catherine. On Wednesday she could spend time with Robert and not feel guilty about it.

He brushed his lips to the tip of her nose. "Good."

Margo told herself to be happy with the promise

of an evening with Robert. But she couldn't help thinking ahead. "It's not going to be easy, is it? I have one free evening a week. That's all."

"Ellie and Peter spend every other weekend with their dad, too, right?"

"Yes, but I'm usually cooking from day to night, stocking up on soups and mixing cookie and muffin dough for the freezer. Then there's the accounting." She rolled her eyes. "And payroll."

Not to mention laundry, housework and spending time with her girlfriends. How did other single moms handle all this and fit in time for romance, too? It was the ultimate question, and Margo still didn't have an answer.

CHAPTER FOURTEEN

ON SUNDAY NIGHT after dinner Robert went through the menu list with Margo. He had a lot of suggestions and Margo decided to implement them right away. Early Monday morning she rewrote the price list on the chalkboard behind the counter. Em arrived for work five minutes before opening.

She made no comment on the new prices, just nodded, then went to the back to grab an apron. Business that morning was brisk as usual and only a few customers complained about the higher prices.

Margo was left with the impression that she could have been charging these prices all along and her volumes wouldn't have been affected, at all.

"I guess you were right and I was undercharging," she admitted to Robert when he came in before lunch.

"The next step is to save money on the cost end. I have some new buying procedures I want to go over with you today. Then tomorrow we'll discuss inventory control."

Margo was open to all of his ideas, but she wasn't as optimistic as Robert about the final result. Whenever Robert spoke of savings, it was half a percentage point here, another half there. Would all these little adjustments add up to enough in the end?

And, more importantly, could she stay in business long enough to get to the point where she was turning a profit?

Midway through the afternoon, Robert received a call and had to leave for another job interview. Margo wished him good luck with mixed feelings. She knew how important it was for him to get back on track with his career. But once he was working fulltime hours again, would they ever find time to spend together?

Singles With Kids friends were coming for a coffee night, and she intended to get their advice on dating. Selena, in particular, seemed able to juggle men as well as her other commitments. Maybe she could help Margo do the same.

In keeping with her new organized lifestyle, Margo served dinner for her children precisely at six o'clock. As she ate, she sorted through the day's mail. Several new bills had arrived and she stuffed them into the basket with the others, without even reading them. One was a second notice with nasty red lettering. She shoved that one to the very bottom.

Robert knew the paltry state of her business bank account balance. She'd admitted that she was using personal savings to pay her bills now, but she hadn't admitted just how quickly those funds were disappearing. She couldn't. She was too embarrassed. Like her friends, Robert had faith in her ability to make a success of the bistro. She couldn't admit to anyone just how desperate the situation really was.

She'd made pasta for dinner—the kids' favorite—and Ellie and Peter both cleaned their plates and asked for seconds. She couldn't even finish her own serving, though. Looking at those bills had upset her stomach. She took a couple of antacid pills, then left the dishes so she could focus on getting the kids organized for bed before her friends showed up. Once homework and baths had been taken care of, she slipped down to the bistro kitchen to bake a pan of caramel brownies for her friends.

Peter and Ellie ran downstairs just when she was pulling them from the Garland's gas oven.

"Can I have a piece?" Peter pleaded.

"I'm sorry, honey."

"But they smell so good…."

"I know." She covered the pan with a clean cloth, feeling like a huge meanie. "But these have way too much sugar. Would you like one of those special lollipops we bought for you?" They were sweetened with sucrose and had been recommended by the nutritionist as a dessert substitute.

But Peter wasn't impressed. He stomped his foot, then raced back up the stairs. Ellie moved in on the brownies. She lifted the corner of the cloth and inhaled the sweet, chocolaty aroma.

"Mom, can I have some?"

Margo didn't know what to say. It didn't seem fair for Ellie to have a treat when Peter couldn't. On the other hand, Ellie wasn't the one with the diabetes. Maybe she shouldn't have baked the brownies at all….

But that wasn't going to be a long-term solution to this problem. She owned a bistro. She baked goodies every day.

"Just a sliver, okay, Ellie? Then please go upstairs and brush your teeth. My friends are coming over for coffee. They should be here any minute."

Margo followed her daughter up the stairs, then once Ellie and Peter were settled for the night, she ran back down to start making coffee. For a change Edward had shown up on time for his shift, and he and Sandy seemed to be getting along well.

Selena was the first to arrive. She was wearing

a dramatic black top with jeans and looked wonderful, except that little white bits of something were stuck to her hair. She glanced around the room. "Wow. Am I early? This is a real first." She perched on one of the stools.

"Espresso?" Margo asked, already scooping a generous quantity of beans into the grinder.

"A double."

"Coming right up." Margo tamped the grounds into the espresso maker, then moved closer to Selena. "What's in your hair?"

Selena patted her head, located one of the tiny white things, then examined it. "Oh, that's Styrofoam from my latest project. I didn't have time to wash my hair after work tonight."

"What are you working on?" Selena's installation art fascinated Margo. The projects were mostly made outdoors and tended to be political statements of one sort or another. As Selena filled her in on the details of this latest undertaking, Margo started work on the other coffees.

Nora arrived just as Margo was putting the finishing touches on her chai latte and Rosie followed right after her.

"Wow, you look great." Selena checked out Rosie's classic black dress, heels and makeup. "Were you at a party?"

"Black tie. Work related, of course." Rosie

made a face. "I wish I'd had time to change, but I didn't want to be later than I already am."

"I don't blame you," Selena said. "Tonight we're going to be talking about Margo's new man."

Margo colored. "I said I wanted to discuss dating as a single parent. Not *my* love life in particular."

Everyone laughed, but Selena said, "We're not letting you off the hook that easily. So where should we sit? Same place as last time?"

"Yes." Margo added whipped cream to Rosie's mocha, then led the way to the annex. "Make yourselves comfortable. I'm just going to grab the brownies from the kitchen."

When she returned, all eyes were on the tray in her hands.

"I have to watch what I eat all week long in order to make up for these nights," Nora said, as Margo set the tray on the table. "Not that I'm complaining, you understand. You're a great cook, Margo."

Margo passed her the knife. "I've always loved baking, but the scent drifts up to the apartment and Peter is feeling really deprived."

"Oh, the poor little guy," Rosie said.

Margo groaned. "I suppose I should try to get all the baking done on the weekends when the kids are with their father, but things always taste better when they're fresh from the oven."

Nora had just tasted a tiny piece of the brownie. She licked her lips then rolled her eyes. "You're not kidding. These are unbelievable. How is Peter making out overall? Besides missing sweets."

"As good as can be expected, I think. He does hate his shots. He likes to hold on to Boy whenever I give them to him. Thank goodness that dog is so gentle."

"Did you ever take him to the vet?" Selena asked.

"I did, and everything checked out fine. The vet gave him a clean bill of health, but she did make one comment that has me a little concerned."

"Oh?"

"She said that Boy still has his puppy teeth. Which explains why he's been chewing everything in sight in our apartment."

"You know what else it means?" Nora said. "That he isn't fully grown yet."

"That's the problem. He's already the perfect size. I wouldn't want him to get much bigger."

"Maybe you should reconsider keeping him. Space issues aside," Nora said, "the last complication you need in your life right now is a dog."

"If only his owner would claim him. I've

always thrived on chaos, but unfortunately juvenile diabetes does not."

Selena reached across the table to pat her hand. "You have my sympathy there. Organization isn't my thing, either."

"I'm far from a perfectionist," Margo added. "But lately my life is definitely verging on out-of-control. Peter's diabetes was the last straw. Or maybe it was the dog. Or—"

"The new boyfriend?" Selena suggested, her eyes sparkling with mischief.

"Yeah," Nora said. "Tell us about Robert."

Rosie laughed. "Those of us with no men in our lives want to live vicariously through you."

"Well, he's wonderful. The only problem is, he's *too* wonderful. I'm thinking about him all the time when I should be concentrating on other things. Like my kids. And my business."

"Careful, Margo." Selena licked a dab of toffee from her pinkie. "I totally approve of the new guy. He looks delicious. But you have to remember... men are just for fun. It's not a good idea to take them too seriously."

"When I first met Robert, I tried to think of him that way," Margo admitted. "As someone I could date occasionally and have a good time with. But after this weekend, I just don't know...."

"What happened this weekend?" Nora wanted to know.

"We spent almost all of it together. *With* the kids. He taught them to play soccer."

"I never introduce men to my son," Selena said.

"Then when do you find time to date?" Margo wondered. "Between work, and looking after a house and spending time with the kids, when is there any extra time?"

"The short answer is, there isn't." Nora scraped a fork over her empty plate. "Not that it's ever been an issue for me. Since Kevin, I can't even picture myself with someone else."

Margo put an arm around her shoulders. "The day is coming when some great guy isn't going to let you get away with that anymore."

"Margo's right. Nora, your day is coming, but Margo's is already here." Rosie cut more slices of brownie for everyone. "If Robert is as special as you make him sound, then you've just got to make room in your life for him."

"If I had any extra hours, I should put them into the bistro."

"What do you mean? This place is perfect the way it is."

"Thanks for saying that, Nora. But it isn't the operations end that needs more time. It's the accounting and reporting side of things."

"You should hire an accountant. One of my physio clients would be perfect…."

"Thanks, but Robert's been helping me out." Not that she could afford to hire an accountant, anyway. "I'm sure we'll have things sorted out soon."

"You've mentioned financial problems before." Rosie gave her an assessing look. "It isn't serious, is it?"

"No. Of course not." Her pride wouldn't let her admit otherwise. Though each of her friends worked in different fields, they were all successful at what they did.

She could not admit that she was anything less. Margo stared at the piece of brownie Rosie had served onto her plate. She wished she felt like eating it. But her stomach was churning again, and she realized she'd been naive to think that her friends were going to be able to come up with a magical solution for her.

There were only so many hours in the day. And only so many dollars in her savings account. It was up to her to make the most of what she had. She'd find some way to make it all work. She just had to.

Friday's Soup of the Day:
Peter Pumpkin Eater

MARGO POURED a refill of decaf for the new mother who'd been frequenting the bistro since her baby was born. Her husband was out of town this week, so she'd been coming in even more than usual.

"I haven't had three straight hours of sleep since he left," the young mother confided. She lifted the cup Margo had just filled. "I wish I could drink the real stuff. But I'm still breastfeeding."

Margo peered at the infant who was sleeping next to her mother's chest. "They're a lot of work," she admitted. "But so worth it. When is your husband coming home?"

"Tonight. I'm planning to say hello, then go straight to bed. And he won't be invited to join me."

Margo laughed, then went to clear a vacant table. She gathered the mugs and plates and carried them behind the counter. It was Friday and since it was the kids' weekend with their dad, she had plans to see Robert. They'd had dinner on Wednesday, and had talked for hours after. He was still optimistic about the bistro's future. The key area right now was inventory control.

The changes Robert had suggested would take a while to implement fully, but even she was feeling more hopeful now.

Next week she'd begin calling her suppliers and see if she could negotiate some of the bulk discounts Robert had suggested.

She kept busy until six o'clock when the night

staff arrived and Margo was able to go upstairs to change. Once she was ready, she pulled out the basket of unpaid bills and added up the amount she'd need to pay everything off. The total exceeded her bank balance by several hundred dollars.

This was what she should be doing tonight. Figuring out how to pay these bills. She still had some money in a retirement fund. If—

The doorbell rang. Robert. She stuffed the basket back onto the shelf, then went to the door. Her stomach was still knotted with worry about the bills, but she had to smile at the sight of Robert in her doorway.

He definitely was the best thing that had happened to her in a long, long time.

"You okay?"

"Sure," she lied, ignoring the sick feeling that lingered in her stomach.

"Sorry I couldn't make it for lunch. What was the soup of the day?"

She smiled. "Peter Pumpkin Eater."

"Pumpkin? I've never had pumpkin soup before."

"It's delicious. I add a dash of curry and coconut milk. It's spicy, but sweet, too. Ellie's envious. She wants me to name a soup for her now."

"Speaking of food, what restaurant do you want to go to tonight?"

She couldn't imagine eating just yet. "Could we take a walk first?" At the word *walk,* Boy perked his ears, but Margo had already taken him out for his exercise. "Sorry, Boy. This time you're staying behind."

Out on the street, Robert took her hand. "Busy day?"

"Very. How about you? I presume the interview went well?"

"The one with Citibank went very well. We talked for hours and I was given the full office tour. But we'll see if I get the call back on Monday."

In the dusk, her familiar street was cast with a romantic glow. Margo noticed there were a lot of couples out walking tonight. She glanced sideways at Robert. Did he think of them as a couple? Had they been seeing each other long enough for that?

They passed a Vietnamese restaurant and Margo inhaled the light scent of lemongrass. Even that delicious aroma wasn't enough to make her hungry.

"Was it just because of your mom that you got into banking?"

"I always knew I would do something in business. I used to follow the New York Stock Exchange the way other boys kept tabs on box scores."

"What a dork you must have been," she teased.

"Ah, but I was a happy dork. How about you? Did you always want to own your own restaurant?"

"I grew up cooking with my mother. She loved preparing big meals for our family and friends and everything she made, she made from scratch. No mixes or shortcuts for her."

"It seems like culinary school would have been a natural fit for you."

"I thought so, too. But my marks were very good and my parents really wanted me to get a college degree. On a lark one year, I took the LSAT, and my scores were so high that everyone encouraged me to continue on with law. My parents were very pleased."

"I guess they would be."

"I met Tom when I was articling. I think working for the same firm masked the fact that we had very little else in common. We definitely had different ideas about the kind of family we wanted to build."

Ahead of them, a line was forming for entrance into one of SOMA's most popular nightclubs. The thumping techno beat ebbed and faded as they passed by. A group of young men casually joined the lineup. One gave Margo an open look of approval.

Robert put his arm around her. "It's getting dark. Maybe we should grab a cab."

She appreciated the protective behavior and knew it was warranted. Certain streets in SOMA were safer than others, and they'd strayed a long way from the bistro.

Ten minutes later, they were in the backseat of a hybrid electric yellow cab headed for Pier 39. Robert had suggested the destination.

"I know it probably seems tacky to you, but I still feel like a tourist, even though I've lived here for a year."

"Pier 39 is always fun," she assured him. "You know there's a carousel…"

He looked at her, amused. "What is it with you and merry-go-rounds?"

"This one is special. Really. It was hand-painted in Italy with scenes of the city's most famous landmarks."

"I assume you're going to want to have a ride?"

"Absolutely. And you're coming, too."

He shook his head.

"Yes, you are. Do you want a horse or a chariot?

Or maybe we should sit in one of the spinning tubs?"

He rolled his eyes.

CHAPTER FIFTEEN

WHATEVER HAD BEEN troubling Margo when he'd picked her up that evening seemed to be forgotten on Pier 39. The place was pure magic as far as Robert was concerned. Or maybe it was Margo who held all the magic.

As they approached the carousel in the middle of the pier, it sparkled with thousands of diamond-like lights.

"Look at that, Robert? How can you resist it?"

"What can I say? I have a lot of willpower." This was true of carousels, but not of Margo. He had no ability to resist her at all.

"Spoilsport." She wrinkled her nose at him, then joined the lineup for tickets.

She insisted on riding, not once, but twice. As before, he was captivated by the sight of her. If only he'd thought to bring his camera...

He noticed a woman taking pictures of her children.

"Excuse me. This may sound strange, but I was

wondering if I could borrow your camera to take a picture." He offered her a ten-dollar bill.

She looked at him like he was crazy.

"You can e-mail me the picture." He pulled an old business card from his pocket and a pen. He scratched out the address of his former place of employment and scribbled down his home e-mail address.

"See that woman?" He pointed to Margo as she whirled by. "Isn't she something?"

Finally the mother smiled, then nodded. "I get it. But you don't need to pay me. It doesn't cost anything to send an e-mail."

She passed him the camera and he thanked God there were still a few romantics left in the world. The next time Margo spun past—smiling, waving, blowing kisses—he snapped a quick shot.

"Thank you," he told the mother, as he passed back her camera. "You've got cute kids."

"You will, too, one day," she predicted.

He thought about Margo's comment that she'd wanted more than two children. "I hope you're right," he told the woman.

She just smiled. The carousel began to slow and she left to find her children.

He waited where he was, not certain if Margo was going to get on for a third ride. But she didn't.

She came running toward him, laughing. "Where did you get that camera?"

He told her the story and she shook her head, still smiling. "That's just crazy. Now you've got to come for a ride with me."

"Real men don't ride toy horses."

"That is so not true."

"Well, this real man doesn't ride toy horses. But I remain happy to watch. Want to go again?"

"Actually, I'm hungry all of a sudden."

"Must be all that spinning around in circles," he joked. If it were him, he'd be looking for the nearest barf bag.

They strolled along the wharf to the Crab House, then perched on stools to eat crab cakes and crab chowder. Robert wondered when he'd last had this much fun.

The answer to that was easy. The last time he'd been with Margo.

After their dinner, he led her away from the crowds. "Had enough walking yet?" he asked.

"Maybe."

He stepped into a shadow and pulled her close. Her body seemed to tremble just a little. "Are you cold?"

"Not at all." She looked up at him with wide eyes and parted lips. He smoothed the hair from her face, then kissed her.

She kissed him back the way she rode merry-
go-rounds—without reservation—and caution
suddenly seemed the most overrated virtue in the
world.

"Margo, would you consider…"

"Yes."

Five minutes later they were in another yellow
cab. This time he gave the driver the address to his
place.

ROBERT'S APARTMENT was neat and organized and
smelled like pine floor cleaner. It was far from the
quintessential bachelor's pad and Margo loved it
for that fact. As soon as he'd locked the door behind them, he started kissing her again, and she felt
the same mad loss of reason she'd experienced on
the wharf.

He slipped off her jacket and his, then started
kissing her again. He paused briefly to ask if she'd
like any wine? Or music?

She said yes to the music, thinking it would buy
her a little time. Was she sure she wanted to do
this? Yes. Was she sure it was smart to do this? No.

But that didn't seem to matter. He turned up the
volume on his stereo and she recognized the hyp-
notic melody of an old Coldplay hit. As Robert
came back to her, she felt the blood rushing, but
it wasn't toward her head.

He cupped her face and kissed her again, and she loved how tenderly he did this. He soothed her body with his hands, and she was amazed at how a touch so gentle could make her feel so hot.

"If I leave the bedroom door open, we'll still be able to hear the music."

For the second time that night she said, "Yes."

But it wasn't the last.

IT WAS ONE IN THE MORNING and Robert had crawled out of bed to make them tea. Margo was curled on her side, with Robert's sheets all around her.

His bedroom was tidy. His sheets smelled like fabric softener. He had a copy of *Find Your Own Parachute* next to the alarm clock by his bed.

"Tea is served." Wearing nothing but a clean pair of boxers, Robert came into the room with a tray piled high with toast and jam he'd brought along with the tea. Ultimate comfort food. She reached for one of the mugs.

Robert crawled under the covers next to her and flicked on the TV. Switching through channels, he paused at a scene between Jimmy Stewart and Grace Kelly.

"Oh, I love that movie."

"Okay. We'll do the Hitchcock thing." Robert picked up his mug of tea, then shifted the tray over to make room for her to snuggle next to him.

Margo made herself comfortable, then reached for a square of toast.

"Thanks for the tea and toast. This is nice."

"Yeah." Robert turned to her. "So was the other."

She smiled. Eventually she sensed him focus back on the television.

After several minutes he asked, "Do they eventually find the wife's body?"

Margo thought for a minute. "You know, I can't remember how it ends."

ON SUNDAY NIGHT Tom brought the children home just after dinner. Usually he dropped them off, then hurried back to his car. Tonight, he stood in the doorway, looking like he had something on his mind.

Margo did not feel inclined to invite him in. "Is there a problem?"

Ellie had raced to her bedroom, while Peter had headed straight for Boy. The two were cuddled on the sofa in the living room. In the background, Margo could hear the cartoon characters from Peter's favorite show having a disagreement.

"You tell me, Margo." Tom leaned a shoulder into the door frame. "Who is this guy you've been dating? He seems to be spending a lot of time with my kids."

"You met him at the wedding, Tom. He's Robert Brookman."

"You introduced him as a friend. I didn't realize you were involved with him."

Margo folded her arms over her chest. "I don't see what business this is of yours."

"Peter told me he started playing soccer with some of the boys at school. I asked him when he learned how to play and he told me 'Mom's friend, Robert, taught me.'"

"So? Do you have a problem with Peter playing soccer?"

"Don't act dumb, Margo. I have a right to know about someone who's spending time with my kids."

"I don't remember being filled in about Catherine when you started seeing *her*."

"So you admit that you're dating? Is it getting serious?"

"You make it sound like it would be a crime if I was."

"Well, are you or aren't you?"

"Tom, lower your voice." Margo glanced down the hall to the family room. Peter seemed oblivious to their conversation, but she couldn't be sure he wasn't listening.

She stepped out to the stairwell and partially closed the door. "Robert and I are friends, let's leave it at that, okay? If we ever decide to get married, I'll be sure to give you a phone call a few days before the ceremony."

Tom's face reddened. "Look, Margo, you can't compare Catherine with this guy of yours. Ellie told me he doesn't even have a job."

"That's enough." She was not going to defend Robert to him. "You're just going to have to trust that the people I bring into our children's lives are good people. Just as I have to trust the same with you."

"But—"

"I'm sorry, but this conversation is over. Say hello to Catherine for me." Margo slipped back inside and quickly shut and bolted the door.

Monday's Soup of the Day:
Poor Man's Vegetable

THE NEXT DAY the credit manager from the bank called to confirm his appointment with Margo. As if she could have forgotten. At about the same time that Robert was meeting the people at Citibank for his second interview, Margo was seated across the desk from a man who looked fresh out of college.

"Unfortunately, according to these numbers—" he patted the cash flow statements "—you're going to have trouble paying off the principal of our loan. In fact, I don't think you'll have enough money to stay in business for another three months."

Three months. Margo swallowed. She'd paid a few of the more pressing bills that morning— her suppliers wouldn't keep up deliveries if her account wasn't current—leaving very little in her savings. She had a meeting scheduled at the bank, where she had her personal account, later in the week to convert some retirement savings into cash. But she was hoping her operating profit would turn around before she needed to spend too much of that.

"A little extra bridge financing right now would pay off for you in the long run." She didn't think the chances were very good that he would say yes, but she had to try.

"Sorry. You're too much of a credit risk for that."

"I'm in the process of implementing some new policies and procedures. I've repriced the menu and tightened my inventory controls." She squared her shoulders and did her best to look dependable. "If you could give me a few months, I'm sure cash flow will improve."

The college graduate referred to the papers on

his desk once again. "I don't think we have a few months."

"How about one month?"

He rubbed his chin as he considered the situation. "Do you really think you can turn this thing around?"

"I've already spoken to a consultant—" surely Robert could be considered one "—and he's assured me that it's possible."

"Well, it would really help us here at the bank if you could get some of these ideas on paper. A business plan, if you will. That, plus a forecast of cash flows as they are expected to be after your implemented changes, might be enough for us to continue with the status quo for the time being."

"Thank you," Margo said, before either of them could change their minds. She left the bank walking tall, but as soon as she stepped outside, her back and her spirits slumped.

Now she needed to come up with a business plan and a forecasted cash flow statement. Could she ask Robert to help? But he'd already done so much and if he landed this new job at Citibank he wouldn't have much free time.

Since it was almost three-thirty, Margo walked from the bank to the kids' school. For a change Ellie was the one in a talkative mood as they walked home.

"Can you make a snack for school tomorrow?" Ellie asked. "For the assembly."

Margo recalled the notice she'd pulled from both of her children's knapsacks last weekend. There'd been a comment about parents providing snacks. She'd made a note on the calendar about it. "Sure, honey. I can put together a fruit tray."

Ellie wrinkled her nose. "I was hoping for brownies."

Margo glanced meaningfully at her younger brother. "You know we're trying to eat more healthfully, Ellie. The fruit tray will have to do." She put a hand on Peter's shoulder. "Are you okay?"

Peter didn't lift his head, just kept shuffling along. "Yeah. I guess."

Since Peter's diagnosis, Margo had substituted fruit and yogurt for the cookies and milk the kids usually ate after school. The fruit and yogurt weren't nearly as popular, though Margo made an effort on the presentation, chopping up the fruit into tiny pieces and layering it with the yogurt in a parfait glass.

At home she set the dishes in front of her children, noting their glum expressions. "Maybe we can play some soccer after dinner— What do you think?"

"Why can't we play now?" Ellie asked.

"You know I have to work until six."

Ellie glared and said nothing.

After their snack the kids went upstairs. "Remember, no TV until after your homework is done," Margo called after them. She did her best to focus on her customers after that, but she couldn't help wondering how much longer she'd be able to do this. How long until the bank pulled the plug on her and she had to admit defeat?

She didn't realize how preoccupied with worry she'd become, until Sandy showed up for her evening shift.

"Margo, are you okay? You look like you've bitten your lip raw."

Margo went to the washroom and checked her face. Her bottom lip did look very red. She applied a thick layer of petroleum jelly, then went back to the kitchen. She took the latest notice from the bank and tucked it behind the phone. Edward came in then to grab his apron.

"How are things?" she asked him. They hadn't had a chance to chat in a while. "Is school going okay?"

"I had to drop one of my classes. No big deal." He tied the apron around his skinny waist, then washed his hands.

It sounded like a big deal to her. She wondered what his parents thought. As far as she knew, he was still living at home. But if he was having trouble at school, that might explain his poor attitude at work lately. Maybe she shouldn't stir up trouble, but she had to ask. "Is work taking up too much time?"

He shrugged.

"Because if you're dropping classes because you're short on time…"

"Hey. Look. I need this job. I need the cash. Everything's cool. Don't worry." He flashed a smile, then headed for the front, where Margo knew he'd do his usual lackluster job.

If she had time to hunt for another employee, she might have called him back and pressed the issue, but she was glad to shelve the problem for later.

Her stomach rumbled, and she realized that this time it was hunger, not nerves. She checked the kitchen clock and was dismayed to see how late it was.

Damn, and she'd been so good about sticking to her schedule lately. Peter must be starving. No time for the planned chicken casserole. She had to make him something quick. Omelets, she decided as she ran up the stairs.

"Peter?" she called as soon as she was inside the apartment.

No answer. The place was eerily silent. She

would have thought the kids would be long finished their homework and watching their favorite
TV shows by now. She went to call them out of
their rooms.

But both were empty.

"Ellie? Peter?" Margo checked the bathroom
and her own bedroom, all with no success. Boy
lifted his head from his cushion by the front window. She bent to give him a scratch. "Where did
they go?"

Boy tilted his head as if to say, *good question.*

Margo straightened, scanning the room for
clues. Could they have slipped outside without
her noticing?

On her way to the front door, she spotted a
piece of paper on the kitchen counter.

Mom, we've gone to the schoolyard to play
soccer.

She sighed with annoyance. What had Ellie
been thinking? They weren't allowed to go out
without an adult and they certainly should have
asked her before leaving the apartment for any
reason.

Really worried now about Peter—not only was
he late for supper, but he was exercising before
a meal, a definite no-no. Margo threw a peanut

butter sandwich together, grabbed a box of juice, then headed for the school. The light was low outside, soon the sun would be setting.

Margo stopped power-walking and started to jog.

She rounded a block of side-by-side Victorians, then came to the grassy field to the south of the school. At first glance she didn't see anyone. Then she noticed two children sitting on the grass next to the sidewalk.

Ellie and Peter. She'd found them.

"Thank goodness you're okay!" She dashed over to them. "Why—?"

She stopped talking when she realized Ellie was propping Peter up. He looked out-of-breath and a little bewildered.

"Mom!" Ellie's voice was full of relief. "Peter can't see right. And he can't walk. He says he's too dizzy."

CHAPTER SIXTEEN

MARGO CROUCHED ON the grass next to her son. She poked a straw into the juice box then brought it to Peter's lips. "Can you drink this, honey?"

His lips parted to accept the straw and his cheeks collapsed as he started to suck. With each swallow, Margo felt her panic ebbing.

"I'm sorry, Mom." Now that help had arrived, Ellie started to cry.

"Don't worry, Peter's going to be fine. But we're going to take him to the clinic just to be sure."

"It was my idea to sneak out and play soccer."

"We'll talk about it later, okay?" Margo scooped her son into her arms. He was so heavy now…in another year she'd never be able to do this.

"I know I should have asked you—" Ellie clung to her side as they started down the sidewalk.

"Shh, Ellie. It's all right." Worried by her son's pale complexion, she tried to walk faster. "Let's just concentrate on looking after your brother. Can you pull my cell phone out of my pocket?"

She had a taxi number stored there and she instructed Ellie on how to place the call while she headed toward the closest main intersection.

"Tell the driver we'll meet him on Mission and Ninth." With Peter's legs wrapped around her hips, Margo held him tight to her chest and focused on her destination rather than the burning in her arms. By the time she'd made it to the meeting point for the taxi, he was looking a little stronger.

"Do you feel any better?"

He nodded.

She hugged him tighter. Ellie reached up to stroke her brother's back.

They waited ten minutes for the taxi, then it took another ten minutes to reach the twenty-four-hour clinic. When Margo described what had happened to the nurse at reception, she and her children were ushered straight to a room.

The doctor was a woman about Margo's age. Margo spewed out their story, her anxiety mounting as she saw the concern in the doctor's eyes. Before Margo finished recounting all the events, the doctor began a physical exam.

"You did everything right," the doctor told her finally. "And since your son's symptoms have receded, now would be a good time to give him that peanut butter sandwich. He needs something substantial, something with protein, that takes longer than the fruit juice to digest."

Margo pulled the sandwich from her purse and handed it to Peter. "Sorry, it's squished."

"That's okay." He gave her a little smile.

As he took his first bite, Margo turned and gave her daughter a hug. Ellie's face was streaked with dried tears.

"I'm s-sorry, Mom."

"Don't blame yourself," the doctor said kindly. "With a new diagnosis of diabetes, situations like this do sometimes occur. It takes time for people to adjust. And it's possible that your doctor's initial treatment plan may need to be modified. Have there been any changes in your routine lately? Is Peter eating differently? Doing any new activities?"

"Soccer," all three of them said at the same time.

The doctor's eyebrows went up.

"A few weeks ago we started playing soccer as a family. And Peter's been playing with kids at school, too."

"Well, then, that could be our answer. Any increase in exercise will require modification to a diabetic's diet and insulin requirements. I suggest you meet with Peter's doctor as soon as possible and discuss all of this with him."

"Yes. I will absolutely do that."

The kids were quiet during the taxi ride home. Margo supposed they were recovering from the shock of the whole frightening experience. At home she let them watch a favorite movie while she made omelets and salad for their very late dinner.

After they'd finished eating, the three of them talked about what had happened. "I don't want you to blame yourself," Margo told her daughter. "Like the doctor said, we can all learn something from this."

After the kids were in bed, Margo poured herself a glass of wine and collapsed on the sofa with the phone in her hand.

Who she really felt like talking to right now was Robert. But obligation had her dialing Tom's number instead.

Catherine answered. "Hi, Margo. How are things with you?"

She sounded genuinely interested, and by now Margo knew her well enough to realize it wasn't an act. "It hasn't been a great day, to tell you the truth. Peter's okay now, but this afternoon he had an insulin reaction."

"Oh, no. That sounds frightening."

"It was. May I speak to Tom?"

"Sure. Hang on."

Margo took several deep breaths while she waited for her ex to come on the line. She'd told the kids that there was no point in blaming anyone for this incident and she'd meant it.

She didn't think Tom would feel the same way, though. And she knew exactly whom he would point his finger at.

Yet, when she explained what had happened, he surprised her by not having much to say.

"You're positive Peter's okay now?"

"Yes. Tomorrow, though, I'm going to call his doctor first thing and see if we need to modify his treatment."

"I'd like to come to that appointment."

"Sure. I'll call you as soon as I know when it will be." Right after Margo disconnected from the call the phone rang again. She pressed Talk and said, "Yes, Tom?" Had he realized that he'd forgotten to berate her for what had happened?

"Sorry. This isn't Tom."

"Robert." She sat up straight, her mind shifting gears rapidly. "How was your job interview today?"

"It went well. Very well." His voice lowered. "How are you?"

They'd spent most of the weekend together but

hadn't spoken since the kids came home from Tom and Catherine's on Sunday night. Margo closed her eyes in an effort to tap into the way she'd felt back then. She loved the fact that they'd watched an old movie together in bed after making love, and before making love the second time. It was a night she would never forget.

The entire weekend had been marvelous.

Robert made her feel cherished and special.

And he'd also distracted her dangerously from all the work that had been waiting for her at home and at the bistro.

"We had a little emergency here tonight," she said lightly, determined not to make it into too big of a deal.

"What happened?"

She only got out the first syllable of her answer before she started to cry. Frustrated with herself, she covered the mouthpiece. Why was she falling apart now? She'd been fine when she was talking to Catherine and Tom.

"I'll be right there," Robert said. Then she heard a click as he disconnected.

FIFTEEN MINUTES LATER, Margo was pouring a glass of wine for Robert. She'd stopped crying only a few minutes before he'd arrived. Though she'd splashed her face with cold water, she knew her eyes were still red and her lips swollen.

"You didn't need to rush over here. I don't know why I fell apart like that."

"I don't know, either," Robert reminded her. "Will you please tell me what happened? You seem fine. The bistro's still standing… Are Ellie and Peter okay?"

She nodded. "They're both asleep. Peter had an insulin reaction tonight. We just got back from the clinic about two hours ago."

Robert's expression softened with sympathy. "That can be very scary."

"The whole thing was terrifying. I came upstairs shortly after seven to make dinner. The kids were nowhere in sight…." She halted, remembering the awful panic of that moment. "When I calmed down enough to look around, I found a note from Ellie explaining that they'd gone to the school grounds to play soccer."

"Are they allowed to take off on their own like that?"

"No. Especially not without asking first." Margo let out a long, pent-up breath then gave him a play-by-play of everything that had happened after that.

Robert drew her in for a hug. "You should have called me."

She'd wanted to. But she and Robert were just on the cusp of something here. She hadn't wanted to presume that he would drop everything to help her.

She sighed as he rubbed his hands up and down her arms. For a moment she laid down the burden of being the one in control and it felt heavenly.

"Poor Margo. What a lousy day."

She pressed her face against his shoulder for another few seconds, then reluctantly drew away. "How about you? Did you hear back from Citibank?"

He didn't say anything at first, but she saw the answer in his eyes. "They offered you the job!"

"Yeah, they did." Finally he allowed himself to smile and she could see how very happy he really was. "I start on Thursday."

Three days from now. "Wow, that's soon."

"It would have been next Monday, but there's a VP in from New York and they want me to meet him."

"Congratulations, Robert. I knew you'd get what you wanted eventually." She glanced at the bottle of Pinot Noir on the counter. "We should be drinking champagne."

Robert pulled her back in close. "And dancing in the moonlight…."

She swayed in his arms. "I like the way you think."

"And I like the way you—"

"Mommy?" A bedroom door opened. "Mom? I can't sleep." Ellie came into the room rubbing her eyes.

Margo had slipped out of Robert's arms with the first sound of her name. "What's wrong, honey?"

"I keep wondering what would have happened if you didn't come to the school and find us. Would Peter have died?"

"Oh, Ellie." Margo took her daughter's hand and led her to the family room. Robert had settled into one of the chairs by the television and Ellie's eyes widened when she saw him.

"I heard talking. I thought it was the TV."

"Robert came over to tell me about his new job."

"Your mom told me what happened today. It must have been really frightening," Robert said.

Ellie nodded.

"Come here, honey." Margo pulled her daughter close to her on the sofa. "I'm glad you didn't stay in your bedroom and worry all alone.

It's good to talk about problems. That's what moms—and dads—are for."

"Your mom is right. You want to know what my mother always told me?"

"What?"

"She said to think about the things that went right. In your case, it was a good thing you left that note for your mom or she never would have known where to find you."

"That's true." For a guy with no kids, Robert's instincts were on the mark. He'd figured out exactly the helpful thing to say.

"And you did something else right, too, Ellie. You stayed with your brother and you held him and talked to him. I bet he would have been really scared if you hadn't been there."

It was bittersweet to see the relief on Ellie's face. Margo hadn't realized how much her daughter had been blaming herself for what had happened.

"I won't sneak out of the house ever again, Mom."

"I know." Margo squeezed her daughter tightly. From his vantage point on the chair, Robert smiled at them, then slowly stood.

"Robert. I'll just—"

"No. You stay there with Ellie. She needs you right now." As he walked by, he brushed the top of Ellie's head and gave Margo a private look. "I'll call you tomorrow."

Still holding Ellie close, Margo watched him leave. They hadn't had a chance to discuss his job and what changes, if any, it would bring to their relationship.

They already had so little time to spend together. Once he was working nine to five again— or more—Robert would no longer be free to drop in for lunch. Or to help her with the business end of the bistro.

She supposed it was selfish of her to think about that. She ought to be glad for him, that he was getting what he wanted. The bistro, after all, was her dream, not his. She'd just have to write up that business plan and revise the cash flow estimates on her own.

TUESDAY MORNING, as soon as the kids were safely at school and she had things under control at the bistro, Margo made her phone calls. The first was to book an appointment with Peter's doctor. The office was able to squeeze them in for later that afternoon. Margo contacted the school to let them know she'd be picking Peter up early, then she called Tom. He agreed to meet her and Peter at the doctor's office.

"I have a meeting that's going to run late on

Wednesday," Tom said. "Is it all right with you if
I take the kids tonight, instead? Peter can come
home with me after the appointment and Catherine will pick up Ellie from school."

"That's fine." Margo spent the rest of the day
in a mad rush. She had to leave Em to handle
things on her own for several hours in order to get
Peter to the two o'clock appointment.

When they arrived at the office waiting room,
Tom was already there, typing messages into his
BlackBerry as he waited impatiently. He did stop
working to give Peter a hug, but Margo was chilled
by the look in his eyes when he glanced her way.

Fifteen minutes later they were invited into one
of the examining rooms. Margo's stomach roiled
as she recalled the anxiety and fear of their previous doctor's trip. Just one month ago, Peter had
been an average, healthy little seven-year-old.

What had happened to change that? Why had
his pancreas suddenly stopped producing insulin?
She wished someone could give her an answer.
The specialists at the hospital had said that no one
knew why some children developed type I diabetes, but she wished she could be certain that
she wasn't somehow at fault. Had she fed him too
many of her homemade sweets? Was that the
problem?

The visit ended up being a full hour and a half,

as they talked to the doctor, then took Peter for more urine and blood tests. He was so brave about getting a needle now, in contrast to just a few weeks ago. He didn't even ask Margo to hold his hand this time, so she remained seated next to Tom.

Her ex sat leaning forward, his hands clasped in front of him, his head bowed. "I can't believe this is happening to Peter."

"I know."

He shot her a glance, again laced with disapproval, and she felt a flare of anger. If they'd been alone, she would have said something, but instead she could only silently fume.

Did Tom really think this was her fault? Didn't he appreciate that this was as hard on her as it was on him?

When the tests were finished, the doctor wanted to speak with them again. He had a few minor modifications to Peter's medical treatment, but mostly he just advised them to be careful to feed Peter an extra snack before exercise and to ensure that he always ate his meals on schedule.

His words hit Margo hard and her anger at Tom evaporated. She realized her ex had been right to blame her. If she'd been with the children, instead of downstairs working at the bistro and if she'd prepared dinner on time, none of this would have happened.

Poor Ellie had been blaming herself all this time, when really it was Margo's fault.

Later, as they all emerged from the building, Tom touched her arm. "We need to talk."

She knew he was right, but she was anxious to relieve Em at the bistro. "How about later tonight?"

"Now would be better."

"I'm sorry, I need to get back to work."

Tom looked annoyed, but after a moment, he nodded. "Okay, Peter, come with Dad."

Margo gave her son a hug. "I'll see you tomorrow after school, okay?"

Peter nodded, an old hat now at the routine of switching between his mother's house and his father's. For a while Margo stood and watched them walk away from her. She felt the old tug of loss and longing…and willed it away. Peter needed his father and she had to learn to let him go.

CHAPTER SEVENTEEN

THE BISTRO WAS A MESS when Margo finally returned. Dirty dishes were strewn over tables and the counter. The garbage was overflowing. Even the La Marzocco was in desperate need of a wipe-down.

Though business seemed to be in a momentary lull, Em was slouched on a stool, drinking a coffee when Margo walked in. She looked totally beat.

"Oh, Em. You've obviously been super busy. I'm sorry I was gone for so long. I'll just grab an apron then be right out." Margo hurried to the kitchen, where she pulled a clean apron from the shelf. She slipped the strap over her neck, tying the belt as she hustled back to the counter.

"How are our supplies? Are we running out of anything?" She squirted soap onto a cloth, then began washing down the espresso machine. After a few moments, she realized Em still hadn't said a word.

Margo stopped cleaning and narrowed her eyes at the other woman. "Are you okay?"

Em slid off the stool to lean against the counter. Her dark hair spilled from the bun that had been so tight and neat at the beginning of her shift. Margo noticed she was no longer wearing her apron. It was balled in her hands.

"Would you like to leave a little early today? By all means…"

Em shook her head.

Not only wasn't she talking, but she wasn't making eye contact, either. Margo felt her stomach shrink into a tight, hard ball. She'd been prepared to lose Edward. In the back of her mind, she had a tentative game plan in place for how to deal with that crisis.

But Em?

Losing Em was unthinkable.

"You've been run off your feet lately. You deserve a raise."

Em sighed. "You can't afford that, Margo."

Margo turned back to Em. "Shouldn't I be the one worrying about what I can afford?"

"I read the letter from the bank that you left next to the phone."

Margo sucked in a breath. She should have been more careful with that letter. Still, she was surprised that Em would have read it. Was it too late for damage control?

"Yes, there have been issues with the bank," she admitted. "But I have the situation under control. This weekend I'm going to prepare my new business plan. Robert's made some great suggestions for how I can improve profitability. All I need is a little time—"

"I wish I could stay and help you buy that time. But I can't go on working with this amount of stress."

"I admit that lately—"

"It's not just lately. It's been crazy since I started. Margo, you're a great person, but your life is just one crisis after another. I keep thinking things will settle down, but they never do."

She was right. Dammit, Em was right. "Maybe if I hire—"

"I hate to be a wet blanket, but we're back to the same problem. You can't afford to hire extra help. I'm terribly sorry. I enjoy working with you and I wish things had worked out differently, but I'm afraid I have to quit."

Quit.

The word sounded cold and hard and horribly final. Margo wanted to cry and beg and plead. But there were tears in Em's eyes. This wasn't easy for her, either. So instead of trying to change Em's mind, Margo held out her arms.

Em was the first to break out of the hug. "I hope you manage to save the bistro. I really do."

So did Margo. "How much notice can you give me?"

"I do have another job lined up, but I can stay for one more week if you like."

Another week. She'd never hire a replacement in that amount of time. But Margo felt too dispirited to argue. "A week will be fine. And why don't you go ahead and leave for the day now. It's quiet. I can handle things on my own until Sandy and Edward show up. Here, I'll take your apron."

Em took her up on the offer and passed over the apron, then grabbed her purse from under the counter. Once she was gone, Margo carried the apron to the back where she tossed it, and the rest of the dirty linen, into the washing machine down the hall. She was just closing the lid when she heard a man's voice calling her name.

She had a wild hope that it was Robert, but when he called a second time she knew better.

It was Tom.

As ROBERT HANDED over his plastic to pay for the new suit, he thought of Margo. He'd been thinking about her all day. And about Peter…and Ellie, too.

He wanted to know how Peter's doctor's appointment had gone and whether Ellie had been able to get to sleep last night. Mostly he wanted to see Margo's face light up at the sight of him, the way it had last night.

"Thank you, sir," the sales clerk said, once he'd signed the Visa form. "We'll give you a call when the alterations are finished."

"Great." He pocketed his wallet, then pulled out the BlackBerry. As soon as he was out of the store, he hit the speed dial for Margo's Bistro, about the fifth time he'd tried today. Again, no answer. He tried not to feel impatient, but he really needed to hear the sound of her voice.

And to tell her what he'd just realized himself… he was in love.

He was wildly, crazily in love with the sweetest, most adorable woman he'd ever met. And now that he had a job, he was finally in a position to help her. With the salary he'd be pulling in, he could become a silent partner in her business. An infusion of cash was exactly what the Bistro needed.

Excited by the idea, he tried to phone her one more time, again with no luck. Dammit, where was that woman?

TOM WALKED THROUGH the bistro right up to the counter until he found her.

"What are you doing here, Tom? Did something happen to Peter?" Margo put the box of detergent back on the shelf, then dusted off her hands.

"He's fine. The kids are with Catherine. I told you I wanted to talk."

He looked pretty serious. After the day she'd had, a hot bath and a glass of wine were what she needed. Not an intense conversation with her ex-husband.

"Well, I can't talk to you until the next shift arrives at five."

"That's fine. I'll wait. Any chance I could get a coffee?"

It wasn't like Tom to be accommodating. It especially wasn't like Tom to be willing to sit around and wait. Full of trepidation, Margo served her ex his coffee, then set to work cleaning tables and running the dishwasher. Soon customers began trickling in again, and business was brisk by the time Sandy arrived.

"Let me know if Edward doesn't show up soon," Margo told Sandy, as she silently prayed that he wouldn't choose tonight to be late or, worse yet, not to show at all.

"Tom?" She went to his table. During the time he'd been waiting, she'd been aware of his frowns, sniffs and sighs. Now she dreaded finding out what was behind all of that. "Why don't we go upstairs for our talk?"

"That's probably a good idea."

She led the way, her stomach in rebellion as she walked down the familiar hall. At the front door she pulled out her key, but found it was unnecessary.

"That's strange." She twisted the knob. "It's open. But I remember locking it this morning." She shot a glance at Tom, who read her alarm correctly.

"Do you think someone's broken in?"

"I guess it's possible."

"No damage to the door," Tom noted. "And I can't hear anyone inside. But just to be sure I should call the police."

Smart plan. But suddenly Margo remembered the dog. Usually he rushed to the front door as soon as he heard their footsteps in the hall. "Boy? Are you there, Boy?"

Nothing.

In alarm, she opened the door. Tom held out a hand to stop her, but she rushed past him into the apartment. At first glance everything was as she had left it that morning. Except for Boy, who wasn't anywhere to be found.

"Margo, are you crazy? A criminal could be hiding in here."

"The dog is missing. I have to find him." Oh, the kids were going to be so upset if Boy had been hurt or was lost. Margo examined the inside of the front door. She could see scratch marks in the paint. As she was kneeling to inspect the damage, the door down the hall opened and her closest neighbor stepped out.

Mrs. Philips was a retired nurse in her seventies. Usually they got along well. They watered plants for each other when they went on holidays and exchanged mail when the letter carrier got things in the wrong slot.

"Margo? I'm sorry about your dog. He was crying and barking for about an hour this afternoon and I just couldn't take it anymore. I used your key and went to check on him."

"I'm sorry he disturbed you."

"Well, I personally don't think pets should be allowed in this building. But regardless, I do feel badly that I let him out. I was just hoping to calm him down. But the second I cracked open the door, he shot down the hall. I guess someone was moving in and our front security door was propped open. I've been out on the street trying to find him, but he's long gone, I'm afraid."

"When did this happen?"

"A few hours ago. I did go down to the bistro to tell you, but you weren't there and the poor woman behind the counter looked so frazzled I didn't dare disturb her. Customers were practically lined up out the door."

Margo slumped against the wall. Boy was out on the street again. She prayed someone kind would find him. She'd have to make up posters... Maybe she could try canvassing some of the closer businesses and residents.

Suddenly she realized her head was aching, as well as her stomach. "Tom, can we possibly talk later? I need to find our dog."

Unbelievably, Tom balked. "This will only take ten minutes. Let me say what I need to say."

She wanted to argue, but if Boy had been missing for hours, ten more minutes wouldn't change much. "Fine."

She ushered him to the family room, then settled in the chair across from his. "Well?"

"This isn't working out, Margo."

She tensed. "Oh?"

"Look, I know you love the kids and you're a good mother at heart. But this restaurant of yours is taking all your time and energy. It was okay when the kids were healthy. But now that Peter's sick, it's just too risky. He needs better supervision. A routine and regular meals."

She felt as if she'd been submerged under water. Tom was talking, but there was a roaring in her ears and tears sprang to her eyes. She wanted to argue, to fight back and defend herself.

But he was right and so was Em. Her life was one crisis after the other. How had she let things spiral so out of control? She'd let Peter down and Ellie, too. She'd tried to juggle it all, and she'd failed.

And now her son was sick, her best employee had quit and the dog was lost.

"Hey, Margo, I didn't come here to blame you. I want to help. I know it's hard work to start a new business, and I never made a secret of my reservations. But if you really want to make a go of it, maybe the kids should start spending more time with me."

Margo felt herself going under again. Disoriented, lost, desperate for air. She'd been expecting him to ask her to give up the bistro. Not her children.

The roaring subsided and she heard Tom say, "Catherine only works part-time. She could drive the kids to and from school. And she'd be there with them when they were home."

If Margo had had one negative thing to say about Catherine, she would have said it right then. But there was nothing. Dammit, she liked Catherine. Catherine was practically perfect. Unlike her.

"Just think, if you had a month or so when you could focus completely on your business—"

"You mean not see the kids at all?"

"Of course not. They'd come to your place Wednesday nights and alternate weekends."

Margo felt tears slipping down her cheeks. Ellie and Peter. She needed to be with them. Needed to tuck them in at night. Needed to do their laundry and laugh at their jokes and be the one they turned to—

Only this wasn't about what she needed.

Tom was right. She had to think of them.

She leaned forward and covered her face with her hands. *Focus, Margo, focus.* Robert believed she could save the bistro if she implemented all of his recommendations. With more time she could write up a new business plan and convince the bank to extend her financing.

Once she had the bistro running profitably, she would be able to hire more help. Spend fewer hours on the floor and more with the kids. Then they would move back home and everything would be so much better.

If only she could live without them for a while.

Could she?

Could they?

Margo took a deep breath. "A week, Tom. They can stay with you for a week."

He looked at her doubtfully. "That won't be enough time for you to get your life organized."

"Yes, it will."

It had to be.

ONCE TOM WAS GONE Margo was tempted to give in to the tears that she'd been fighting. But she was afraid that if she started, she wouldn't be able to stop.

And there was simply too much she had to do right now.

She had to hire someone new for the bistro. Find Boy. Prepare the business plan. Pay the bills.

Pack a suitcase for Peter and Ellie.

Despite her efforts, she felt fresh tears sting her eyes. The kids had lots of clothes and toys at their father's place, but there were some favorite things she knew they would want if they wouldn't be home for a week. She'd promised Tom she'd bring their things to his house later that night. In turn, Tom had agreed to wait to talk to them about the change in plans until she was there to do it with him.

First, she called downstairs and asked Sandy to keep an eye out for the dog. Sandy promised she would get Edward to check the neighborhood, too. "He might as well do that," Sandy said, "since he doesn't do much else around here."

Margo made no comment, but she knew Sandy was right, and that she had more employee troubles waiting around the corner.

Once that had been organized, Margo went to Ellie's room and began gathering the clothes and books she guessed her daughter would want. Adding each item to the suitcase was torture. Despite the fact that the separation was only temporary, only for a week, Margo felt as if her kids were being torn from her.

She couldn't help but hope Peter and Ellie wouldn't want to stay with their father. If they insisted on coming home after school tomorrow, as previously arranged, she would move heaven and earth to make it work.

Once the suitcase was ready, she tossed it into the trunk of her car, then headed for Pacific Heights. She arrived just around the kids' bedtime and Ellie and Peter were already bathed and in their pajamas. Catherine was reading them a chapter from *Charlotte's Web.*

Margo swallowed down a lump at the perfect picture her children made with Tom's new wife. When was the last time she'd read to the kids together?

In the end Tom did the talking, because Margo knew if she said one word, she'd end up bawling. As it was, she had to duck her head to hide her tears when the kids reacted calmly to their father's suggestion that they stay with him for the next week.

"It'll be nice to be here a little longer for a change," Ellie said.

"But what if I miss Mom?" Peter wasn't quite as brave.

Margo gathered all her strength. "You can phone me whenever you want. And if you really miss me, I can come for a visit."

"I guess." Peter wiggled off the sofa. "Can I play computer games before bed?"

"I'm sorry, Peter," Catherine said calmly. "We'd agreed on one chapter and then bed, remember?"

"Oh, yeah." Peter was about to run off, when Margo called him back.

"Can I have a kiss?" She tried not to cling when he came to her. Smiling had never been more work in her life. "I'll talk to you tomorrow, honey. Sleep tight."

Then it was time to say goodbye to her daughter. She could see the questions in Ellie's eyes. She wasn't quite as accepting as her younger brother.

"It's only for a week, right, Mom?" she asked as Margo hugged her.

"Only a week," Margo promised, forcing herself to break off the hug after several seconds.

She left without saying anything else. She simply couldn't. Ellie's comment kept playing through her head. Did her kids both wish they could spend more time at their father's house? What if, after the week was over, neither one of them wanted to move back in with her?

CHAPTER EIGHTEEN

MARGO NEEDED HELP, and Robert was the first person she thought of. She longed to cry on his shoulder, to ask for his help with the bistro, to talk to him about her fear that she was going to lose her children completely.

But she resisted the urge to call him. She felt horribly guilty that she'd fallen in love at a time like this. How could she have done that when her children and her business were already suffering from lack of attention? Her relationship with Robert was the height of selfishness. Despite the advice of her friends, this was not the time in her life for romance.

Margo made a pot of coffee, then grabbed a pad of paper. She searched for business plans on the Internet, found something that would work as a template, then used Robert's notes to fill in the blanks.

She did okay with the written analysis part. But when it came time to prepare the forecasted cash flow statements—the numbers that would show just how profitable her business would be after she implemented all the changes—she was stymied. If only she had at least a basic amount of accounting knowledge.

Just before ten o'clock, her phone rang. Worried there might be a problem with the kids, she reached for the receiver. It was Robert.

"Hey, Margo. Did you get my messages?"

It was scary how good the sound of his voice felt.

"I haven't checked the machine." She'd wanted to. But she'd been afraid there would be a call from him on it and that she'd be too weak not to phone him back.

"I was hoping I could come over after the kids were in bed. Maybe have a coffee. Is it too late?"

She steeled herself against the temptation to be with him. "I've already had two cups tonight."

There was a hesitation before he answered. "Are you all right? Are you upset with me over something?"

"I'm fine and, no, I'm not upset." It wasn't really a lie. She wasn't upset. She was devastated.

"Are the kids okay? How was Peter's doctor's appointment?"

"The appointment was fine and so are the kids." She hesitated. "Actually they're at Tom's tonight. He switched nights because of a business meeting."

"So you're alone?"

"Yes." Tonight and the next seven nights. She clenched her teeth, still not sure how she was going to stand it.

"What if I came over with a bottle of wine?"

She wanted so badly to say yes, to spend a few delicious hours not worrying about her problems. But her responsibilities had reached the point where they simply couldn't be ignored.

"I'm busy, Robert. I'm working on a report for the bank."

"I could help."

Again Margo hesitated. She so wanted to say yes. He'd be able to do those darned cash flow statements much easier than she could. But if she accepted his help, she'd be tacitly encouraging their relationship. And that was something she could no longer do.

"That's okay. I think I can handle it. Speaking of which, I'd better get busy. Good luck with your first day at the new job."

The cheerfulness in her voice was all fake, and she hoped Robert didn't pick up on it. If he knew how much she cared about him, how much she wanted him, he'd be right over here.

And she couldn't let him do that. It wouldn't be

fair to him. Not when she'd decided that it was time to end things between them. It wasn't something that could be said over the phone, but the next time she saw him, that was exactly what she had to do.

Employed

ON THURSDAY MORNING Robert sank into his new office chair and planted his hands on the smooth wood desk. He looked around, feeling like a king surveying his domain. Even though it was a relatively small domain, it was still his. This was his desk, his computer, his little corner of the San Francisco banking world.

He picked up the brass nameplate that hadn't yet been positioned on the wall by his workstation. Robert Brookman, Director of Commercial Banking. That was *him*.

Earlier, he'd had coffee with his managing director and the other members of his team. He'd been introduced to the visiting New York VP and had been given an office tour by Gloria in HR.

On his desk were several piles. One contained company manuals on everything from lending limits to standards for documentation. In another pile were the forms Gloria had given him. He had to get signed up on payroll and there were some for the health and dental program. Then there were the retirement savings plans and automatic monthly deductions for a charity of his choice.

But what Robert was most excited about was the form to order new business cards. He could hardly wait to have them in his wallet and suit jacket again.

Using the new Montblanc pen he'd purchased yesterday, Robert went through the paperwork methodically. In the afternoon he was meeting with the IT guys, who would introduce him to the bank's various software packages, including client management systems, product packages and reporting templates.

His prospects had never looked brighter. In five years, *he* would be the vice president that new employees would be brought in to meet.

He sighed deeply with satisfaction. He was back in his element, in the world where he belonged.

At noon, his new boss came to check on him. "We were hoping to take you out for lunch, but several of the guys on our team are out on meetings this afternoon. Okay with you if we do the welcome lunch tomorrow?"

"Sure. Tomorrow is great." The words were no sooner out of his mouth, than his boss disappeared down the hall. Robert recorded the appointment in his BlackBerry. One of the guys he'd met that morning—Darren? Darryl?—showed up next.

"A couple of us are heading to the Plaza for lunch. Want to come?"

Robert hesitated. It would be good to get to know his coworkers, but Margo had sounded so strange on the phone the other night and he hadn't heard from her since, even though he'd called again yesterday, several times. He knew he'd feel better if he could see her in person and make sure everything was okay.

"I've got something to take care of today," he told Darren-Darryl. "I'll catch you next time, okay?"

"Sure thing."

Robert slipped his BlackBerry into his pocket, then made his way through the corridors, smiling and nodding at the people he met along the way. Soon these people would be familiar to him. This place, with its thick carpet and earth-toned walls and muted art, would feel like a second home.

Looking forward to that day, Robert waited with a group of others for the elevator. They piled on together, at least ten of them, and made their stop-and-go descent to street level. Outside he hailed a cab and prayed for moderate traffic.

Twenty minutes later, he was standing in front of Margo's Bistro. The soup of the day was

Squashed Pear. He thought of the first time he'd walked by this place, how the aroma of that soup had pulled him in.

And how Margo had drawn him back, again and again.

He hadn't admitted the truth to himself at first. He'd pretended it was the soup, the scones, the rich and flavorful coffee. But really it had been the bubbly blonde behind the counter who had touched him. He couldn't wait to see her now, to tell her all about his first morning at work.

To tell her that he loved her….

But a young woman he'd never met before was working behind the counter with Em. He waited in line, then ordered his usual. "So where's Margo?" he asked, as he dug for change in his pocket.

"She's in the kitchen, baking," Em told him, as she slid the bowl of soup across the counter. "She wants to start offering a broader selection of desserts and quick breads."

"Really?" He was pleased to hear it. Her profit margins were largest on those items she made from scratch. Obviously she was wasting no time in putting his recommendations into place.

Robert took his food to his usual table. One thing about sitting at the back, the table was usually available when he wanted it. Quickly, he ate his meal, hoping that Margo would come out front for a bit.

When his food was gone and she still hadn't shown up, he decided to check on her. He pushed on the kitchen door and found her kneading dough at the counter. A wisp of hair dangled over one eye. Though she looked pretty, as usual, he thought she seemed tired.

"Robert. Aren't you supposed to be at work?"

"I am. Or at least I was. I'm on my lunch break right now. What's this?" He picked up a crumb from the empty bowl and tasted it. "Sweet."

Margo sighed. "It's something new I'm trying. I've set myself a goal of increasing revenues by five percent this month."

"That's great. Want me to price the margins for your new recipes?"

Margo's face turned pinker. "That's okay. I can handle it."

Something was definitely wrong. The Margo he'd come to know and love was warm and giving and adorable. Now she looked as if she'd pull out a can of mace if he tried to give her a hug.

He decided to push a little harder.

"I was wondering if we could go out for dinner this weekend? Maybe watch another movie?" He watched closely for her reaction, hoping against hope that he was reading her wrong and that she would give him one of her glorious smiles.

But she didn't. "I'm so busy right now, Robert. I'd like to, but I can't."

"Something's different." He studied her face, trying to figure out what it was. "You've always been busy, but the bistro isn't open twenty-four hours a day and you do have staff. What's up…is there a problem with the kids?"

"Sort of." She kept her eyes downcast. "Tom thinks I've been neglecting them. They've gone to live with him and Catherine for the week."

"What?" He couldn't believe it. "Why?"

"To give me time to get things turned around here." Her voice lowered. "And because what happened with Peter the other day was my fault."

"Margo, that's preposterous." She couldn't really think that.

"If I hadn't been working, they never would have been able to sneak out of the apartment."

"You can't keep kids under constant surveillance. Whether you'd been working down here, or cooking a meal upstairs or making the bed in your room…if they wanted to go badly enough, they would have found a way. Besides, kids do break the rules now and then. It's not automatically their parents' fault."

Suddenly he saw that the lines around her eyes weren't just from exhaustion. She'd been crying.

"Stop working for a minute. Talk to me."

Her mouth tightened. "I can't. Don't you see? I've got one week to turn this place around. So this isn't a good time for me to be…seeing someone."

"Don't push me away. I can help." He loved her. He wanted to tell her that. But he had a sick feeling it wouldn't make any difference.

"You've got your new job to worry about. I know how much it means to you. You don't have time to help me out here. You know you don't."

"Maybe not right this minute. But later—"

"Later isn't going to work. When I'm not working, I need to be with my kids. It's that simple."

He couldn't believe this. "So what are you saying? You can't take any time for yourself?"

"Don't be ridiculous. Of course I can take time off. Half an hour here. Ten minutes there. Do you honestly think that would be enough for you?"

He stared at her. Honestly, no. "But—"

"My kids have to come first. Please understand that."

He did. He really did. And yet, her decision still felt wrong to him. Somehow he had to persuade her that with his help they could make it work.

Unfortunately, though, his lunch break was almost over, and he couldn't be late on his first day on the job. "I have to get back to the office. But Margo, this isn't the end of things. We're going to talk again. And soon."

CHAPTER NINETEEN

Soup of the Day: Ellie-gant Vichyssoise

MARGO WROTE the soup of the day on the chalk-board with a heavy heart. It was Sunday and her kids had been living with Tom and Catherine for five days now. She called them every day and they seemed to be doing fine. They'd never once asked if they could see her before their next scheduled visit—which wasn't until Wednesday.

It had been the longest five days of her life.

Margo went back to the kitchen to empty the trash. When she took the garbage bag out to the lane, she was amazed to find Boy sitting there as if he'd been waiting for her to show up.

"Boy? Is that you?"

As soon as he heard her voice his tail wagged madly and his entire body shook.

"Where have you been, you crazy dog?" Margo dropped the bag of trash and wrapped her arms around the puppy.

He cocked his head to one side, as if he was as puzzled by his errant behavior as she was. But at least he'd come back. At least he was safe.

The little guy was dirty and obviously starving. After feeding him, Margo took him to the doggy wash before letting him into the apartment. As soon as he'd run in the front door he checked out both kids' rooms, then settled into his bed and fell promptly to sleep.

It was great to have him home, but Margo couldn't help wondering if he'd run away in the first place because he hated being cooped up in a small apartment all day. Maybe it wasn't fair to the dog to keep him here any longer.

Margo dropped to the floor next to the doggy bed and tried not to look around her. The place was a mess. When was the last time she'd taken the vacuum out? On the desk sat her incomplete business plan. She had to get that finished and to the bank.

But all she could think about were the two empty beds in the rooms down the hall.

And Robert. Dammit, why was he still in her brain, using up valuable thinking time when she'd already decided that their relationship had to end?

He'd probably come to the same conclusion. He hadn't called since Thursday.

Margo tried to summon the energy to attack

the business plan. But when Boy shuffled over to rest his head on her lap, she found herself wrapping an arm around him and staying exactly where she was.

She'd grown to love this guy and so had the kids. But—there was no denying he was a complication they just didn't need right now.

She reached for the phone on a nearby table and dialed Selena. When there was no answer, she tried Nora.

"Margo? What's up?"

She hadn't planned on falling apart. But hearing the concern in Nora's voice, everything just came gushing out. "My life is a disaster. Nora, it's been a terrible week. On top of everything else, I lost the dog and now I've found him again and I'm realizing that I just can't cope with looking after a pet in this apartment."

"It's okay, Margo, calm down. Maybe you're right. Maybe giving the dog to Selena and Drew would be the smartest thing."

"I just tried to call her but she isn't home right now. Do you think she still wants a dog?"

"I'm sure she does."

"Do you know when she'll be home? I'd like to give her the dog before the kids come home. I think it'll be easier that way."

"But won't the kids need to say goodbye?"

"I'll ask Selena if they can come to her house to do that. I think it will be good for Ellie and Peter to see him in his new home and to know that he's happy."

"That makes sense. How about I come and pick him up right now, then? I'll get him to Selena as soon as I can find her."

"That would be wonderful, Nora. Thanks so much." If Boy spent so much as one more night in her house, she wouldn't have the strength to say goodbye to him.

"No problem. Don't give it another thought. Now is something else wrong? You've been crying, I can hear it in your voice."

"Oh, Nora…" Pride didn't seem so important to Margo now, when she considered all she'd lost and all she still stood to lose. "I'm in trouble with the bank. I can't meet my loan payments."

"Do you need money? I had no idea the bistro wasn't doing well. You always seem so busy."

"Yes, I know. Apparently revenue isn't all you need to turn a profit. You also need to control your expenses."

"I thought Robert was helping you with that."

"He was. Not anymore."

"Why?"

"Well, I kind of broke things off with him."

"You didn't?"

"I had to. Falling in love takes time and energy and I don't have either of those."

"But you seemed so happy with him."

Margo bit her lip to try and stop herself from breaking down in tears. Nora was right. She *had* been happy with Robert. But that hardly seemed to matter anymore. "I haven't told you the worst of it. Tom came to see me last week. He was worried about Peter. About both of the kids."

"Because of Peter's reaction the other day?"

"Yes." Margo rubbed her forehead with the heel of her hand. If only this aching would stop. "The kids have gone to stay with Tom and Catherine. We've said it's just for a week, but I'm afraid it may be for longer."

"What?" Now Nora really sounded shocked. "Why?"

"Because I'm a mess."

"That's not true."

Though Nora spoke in her defense, Margo heard a hint of doubt in her voice, and it occurred to Margo that she *really was* a mess and all her friends, as well as Tom, could see it.

She was giving up the dog and giving up Robert, but maybe that wasn't enough.

When she thought about what was really important, what mattered more than anything, the answer was clear: her children. She couldn't risk losing them. Nothing would be worth it.

Including the bistro.

WHEN NORA DROPPED BY to get Boy, she stayed for tea. She tried to talk Margo out of giving up the business, but the more they discussed the matter, the more convinced Margo became that she was making the right decision.

That night Margo hoped she would finally feel at peace, but she woke up the next morning with her stomach still in knots, her head still aching.

Nevertheless, she carried on with her plan. First she called Em and told her of her decision. They weren't going to open this morning, or any other morning. Em should feel free to start her new job immediately.

Out of habit, Margo went downstairs anyway. She touched the sign on the door, the Open sign she normally flipped over every morning at eight. Today the sign would stay where it was for the first time in the twelve months since she'd opened this business.

Margo imagined customers—regulars and semiregulars and mere passersby—walking toward her shop with anticipation, only to be met with a locked door and a sign that told them nothing except that the bistro was closed. They'd all need to get their morning snack and coffee somewhere else now.

She hated knowing that she was going to disappoint those people. Hated thinking that never again would she stand behind the counter of her very own restaurant and serve food that she had made with her own hands to the friends and neighbors she'd grown so attached to.

Next Margo went to the kitchen. Yesterday she'd set out the recipes she'd planned to make this morning. There was the one for Sherry Chanterelle soup, and the morning glory muffins and herb and cheese scones. She filed the recipe cards away, along with the notebook she used to develop new recipes. Those cherry, chocolate and pecan muffins just didn't seem very important anymore.

She made herself coffee and, fortified with caffeine, took the next difficult step: finding a job. She called Henry Kovatch and when she ended up on voice mail, she spoke quickly, wanting to commit herself before she could chicken out.

"Harvey, this is Margo Evans. I'm looking to go back to work and I was wondering if you have room in your firm for another family lawyer. Here are my numbers." She recited them for both her home and cell phones, then hung up and began looking for the card from the realtor who had leased this space to her.

Another voice mail. Why was it, when she finally decided to make one of the most important—and heartbreaking—decisions of her life, no one was in to take her calls?

She left a message with the Realtor, then sat back to gather her strength.

What she really wanted to do right now was talk to Robert. She longed to discuss her decision with him and get his point-of-view. A hug would go down really nicely right now, too. But she knew she had to stick with her plan.

It would all turn out for the best. She'd go back to a regular job with regular hours. Soon she'd be able to afford a house with a backyard and she'd be able to buy another puppy for the children. Giving up everything else would be worth it.

From the day Tom had told her of his plans to remarry she'd resented him for the perfect new life he'd managed to build from the ashes of their failed marriage.

Now she was going to make a perfect new life for herself and the children, too. If Ellie and Peter needed stability and security, then that was exactly what Margo was going to give them.

As for Catherine, Margo knew what she had to do.

She headed back to the kitchen and instead of starting the baking for the business, she whipped up a double batch of the kids' favorite oatmeal cookies. Shortly after lunchtime, when she knew Catherine would be home from work, she drove to Pacific Heights.

Catherine was still in her business suit when she opened the door. "Hi, Margo." She looked surprised but was too polite to say anything about the unexpected visit. "The kids aren't home from school yet."

"I know. I was hoping to have a minute with you." Margo offered her the basket. "I want to thank you for all you've done for my children. Just last night I was thinking how lucky the kids and I are that Tom married someone as nice as you."

Catherine's eyes widened, then gleamed with sudden tears. "They're great kids."

Margo heard the sincerity in her voice and knew that she was doubly blessed. So easily Tom's wife could have resented her children. Instead, Catherine's heart embraced them.

"Those are Peter and Ellie's favorites," she explained. "I've included the recipe."

"Thank you. Would you like to come in for some tea? I don't need to pick up the children for a few hours."

Margo forced a smile. "Another time, okay?"

On her way back to the car, with her head still

pounding and her stomach hurting and her heart aching, Margo wondered when she was going to start feeling like she'd made the right decision.

ROBERT FELT alternately restless and angry all week long. Despite being a reasonably intelligent man, he'd gone and made the same mistake twice—fallen in love with a single mother.

Two Saturdays after Margo had told him she didn't want to see him anymore, Robert went for a long, aimless walk. After about an hour he found himself passing by Belinda's apartment. He went to a nearby shop for a milk shake and when he stepped out to the street again he happened to catch the three of them—Andrew, Belinda and Belinda's new boyfriend—on their way home from some activity that had given them all a touch of sun on their faces. They looked tired as they made their way into the apartment foyer.

Neither Belinda nor Andrew noticed him standing at the ice-cream shop across the road. As the boyfriend held the door open, he placed a hand on Andrew's shoulder. The gesture seemed easy and natural. Andrew turned slightly and Robert glimpsed a smile on the boy's face.

He looked happy.

So maybe Belinda's decision for Robert to just butt out had been the right one in the end. Robert studied the woman he'd thought he loved. He remembered how he'd felt when she'd told him she'd found someone else. His first thought had been for Andrew.

That hadn't happened with Margo. Much as he liked her kids, his first thought had been for her. He loved her in a way he'd never loved Belinda. He'd felt the magic the first time he'd stepped into her bistro.

He couldn't let that go.

Robert started walking again, this time purposefully. Soon he was on her street. Even before he reached the bistro, he knew something was different. The air didn't smell right.

A Closed sign hung over the door. He peered through the glass. The space was dark and empty.

He stood back and noticed another sign, this one in the window. It was a local Realtor's sign.

Robert swore. What was going on here? He tried knocking on the locked door, then when that didn't yield any response, he went to the main entrance for the second-floor apartments. He punched in the code for Margo's apartment and waited until her answering machine kicked in.

"Leave a message."

"Hey, Margo, it's me, Robert." He had more to say, a lot more, but it seemed crazy to try and put all of it on an answering machine. "I'll come by later."

He pulled out his BlackBerry and tried her cell number. No luck.

Robert knew he wouldn't be able to focus on anything else until he found out what had happened to her. He returned to the street, and sat on the apartment stoop. Who else could he call? He knew Em fairly well, but had never been introduced to her formally so he had no idea of her last name.

What about the friends Margo met for coffee? Nora Clark. Didn't he have her business card somewhere? He went through his wallet and found the card she'd given him the night they'd met.

Fortunately he caught her between clients.

"Do you know where Margo is? She isn't answering her home phone or her cell."

"I think she and the kids are looking for a new house."

What? "Why is the bistro closed?"

"Margo's selling it. She started back with a law firm last week."

"She's going to work as a lawyer again?"

"That's right. Unfortunately she wasn't making money with the bistro. At least not enough to pay down her bank loan."

Oh, Margo. He'd known that sending the kids

to their father—even temporarily—had been torture for her. He should have realized it would push her to the breaking point. Why hadn't he insisted that she let him help her?

"Nora, I think Margo's making a big mistake here."

"So do I. The bistro was a really special place. I can't believe it wasn't profitable."

"It could have been." She'd been so close. Robert sucked in a frustrated breath. Any food service business that did the volume of sales that Margo's had would turn a profit if properly managed. Why hadn't she come to him before giving up on it?

There were two possible answers.

Because Margo didn't love him and didn't want his help. Maybe she'd worried that if he became too involved in her business, she'd be obliged to him in some way.

But there was another possibility that Robert liked better. That Margo *did* love him. And that she'd been too proud to admit that she couldn't handle everything on her own.

If the second answer was right, then he still had hope. Of course he would need to take some pretty big risks…emotional as well as financial.

Should he chance it?

He thought about the way he felt every time he

stepped foot into Margo's Bistro and he knew he couldn't live without that feeling in his life.

"Nora? I have an idea. But I'm going to need some help…."

CHAPTER TWENTY

Margo handed a box of Kleenex to the woman sitting across from her at the small meeting table. Her client was in her early thirties, a wisp of a woman, temporarily overwhelmed by her circumstances.

"I'm sorry," Lisa Scott whispered, dabbing her eyes with a tissue.

"No reason to be sorry. I know this is very hard."

Lisa nodded. "Our son is only eight. And nothing I say will convince Brad that he's setting a terrible example."

"If you can't reason with him, then you should try mediation. It's been helpful for many couples I've worked with over the years." Margo passed Lisa a business card. "You may have someone else in mind, but I have no hesitation in recommending Audrey Dodds. She's very warm and caring, but she can be firm, as well."

Lisa accepted the card. "That sounds like exactly what I need."

Their meeting was over, and Margo offered Lisa a drink of water before walking her back to the reception area. She was glad this was her last appointment of the day. This meeting had been more grueling than she'd anticipated.

Margo went back to her office to enter her notes into her computer. As she recorded the behavior Lisa had found so objectionable in her ex—in particular having women over for the night when his son was staying with him—she reflected again on how fortunate she was that Tom had married someone like Catherine.

She was lucky in many ways. Lucky that she had qualifications for a well-paying job. Lucky that her kids were resilient and strong. Even lucky that she'd been able to sell the restaurant to someone who intended to operate it as a going concern. As well as subleasing the building space, she'd received value for her leasehold improvements and existing assets. The papers had been signed last night, all transacted through numbered corporations in order to limit liabilities.

She knew she should be grateful she'd ended up getting enough money so that she could clear her outstanding business loan, plus afford first and last month's rent on the house she and the kids had looked at last week.

It wasn't as grand as Tom and Catherine's house in Pacific Heights. But there were three bedrooms and a study and a big backyard. The kids hadn't seemed as excited about it as she'd expected. It seemed as if they'd been fond of that crazy, cramped apartment after all. But over time they'd get used to the bigger house. They all would, she hoped.

Compared to Lisa Scott—heck, compared to the vast majority of her clients—she had nothing to complain about.

After typing in the last comment, Margo closed the document then shut down her computer. With a sigh, she gathered her briefcase and jacket for the commute. The kids were at their father's tonight. She and Tom had come up with a new coparenting plan, one where the kids alternated weeks between each home.

It wasn't the perfect solution, but it seemed to be working more smoothly than their previous schedule. The kids weren't shuttled around quite so much, and they seemed to appreciate that.

At any rate, it was good that they weren't going to be around while she finished up the packing. Tomorrow the movers were coming. It was going to be a long, difficult day.

The hardest part of all of this, Margo thought, was walking past the Closed sign on the bistro door. It was something she'd been doing every day now for almost two weeks. Something she would do once more tonight, then again tomorrow then never again….

Tears burned behind her eyes as she stepped into the elevator. When her cell phone rang, she scrambled to answer the call. "Hello?"

"Margo. It's good to hear your voice."

It was Robert. Margo stepped off the elevator, heart pounding and knees uncharacteristically weak.

"I was wondering if you would meet me for coffee?"

She closed her eyes against the rush of longing she felt to say yes. She'd given up so much to get her life back on track for her children. Letting the bistro go had been bad enough.

But Robert.

She'd had no idea how much she would miss him.

"Just coffee, Margo," he said quickly, as if he could sense her indecision and was trying to tip the scales. "Just fifteen minutes of your time."

How could she deny him that, especially when her kids weren't even waiting at the after-school day care program for her to pick them up.

"Yes." She could feel her lips turning up in a smile. "Where?"

He hesitated. "I have a place in mind, but it's complicated to explain. How about I meet you at your apartment in a half hour?"

She ought to be able to make it by then. "Sure. I'm just leaving the office now." She paused for a beat. "Thanks for calling, Robert."

"You bet."

AS SHE ROUNDED the corner of her street, Margo saw Robert waiting for her on the sidewalk. She was five minutes early so she hadn't expected him yet.

He'd come from work and was dressed in a suit. His hair was short again. He must have had a trim. Margo thought back to the first time she'd met him. She'd thought he looked a little too conservative then.

But he looked perfect to her now.

He smiled and she started walking faster. She couldn't believe how much better she felt at just the sight of him. They had so much to talk about. She wondered if he would be glad to find out she was working as a lawyer again. Maybe, just maybe…

She pushed herself to go even faster, cursing the heels she'd paired with her pantsuit that morning.

"Margo." Robert stepped toward her, gave her a hug then stepped back to look at her. "You look great. Very professional."

"Thanks. You look good, too. How's work going?"

"Very well. I think it was a good thing I lost my job at Wells Fargo. This new position is right up my alley."

With the first excitement at seeing him passed, Margo took in her surroundings. Something didn't seem right....

"What's that smell?"

Robert grinned. "Are you referring to the soup of the day?"

"What are you talking about? Robert, I closed the bistro. Didn't you see the sign?" Surely the new owners hadn't reopened already?

She walked up the street to point out the Closed sign to him, but it was gone and the door to the bistro had been propped open. The chalkboard in the window proclaimed "Store-bought Tomato" as the soup of the day.

Store-bought tomato? What kind of idiot had subleased this space from her? She went inside. Nora and Selena were behind the counter serving a long lineup of customers.

"What's going on here?"

Robert came up from behind her. "Meet the new owner of Margo's Bistro."

"Nora and Selena are the new owners?"

"No." He put his hands on her shoulders then swiveled her around. "Me." He rattled off a number, and Margo realized it was the company number from the lease.

"*You're* the new owner?"

Robert nodded.

"I need to sit down."

"There's a table at the back that comes highly recommended."

She let him take her arm and lead her there. Her friends were so busy they paid no attention to her, at all. "This doesn't make any sense. Nora and Selena have jobs. Why are they here?"

"They've been helping me out. As has your friend Rosie, and Sandy and Edward. But we are more than ready to hand the reins back to you. I'm afraid the scones were rock-hard today. And the canned tomato soup is definitely not catching on. The muffins were a hit though."

"Muffins? What kind of muffins?"

"Come to the kitchen and I'll show you."

It felt strange having Robert lead her to the kitchen instead of the other way around. He picked up a muffin from the counter and broke off a corner for her.

Margo chewed. Delicious flavor. Perfect texture. And the little something extra that had been missing last time was now present.

"You perfected my cherry-pecan-chocolate muffins?" Somehow this one thing, more than anything else, astonished her. "How did you do that?"

"I followed your notes. Including the addition you made the last time. I never would have thought of adding—"

"Shh." She put a finger to his mouth. "All my recipes are secret you know." She tried another taste. "These really are great."

"They sold like crazy. Tomorrow you'd better bake a double batch."

She shook her head. When had he done all this? Reopened the place, organized the staff, restocked the kitchen and baked the darn muffins?

Last night the Bistro had still been closed, so he must have reopened it early this morning. How incredibly sweet, but...

"Where did you get the money?"

"I have connections," Robert reminded her.

Oh, yeah. Citibank. Good connections.

"But *why*, Robert? I appreciate the thought, so much, but I can't come back to the bistro. It isn't financially viable. I tried, but I just couldn't fix things."

"Do you really think you belong in a law office? Tell me honestly. Is that what you want?"

She couldn't face him. "That isn't the point. Sometimes we have to make sacrifices—"

"But why? Margo, I know we can make a go of this business. And I also know your children would rather live here with you than in some postcard-perfect two-story house."

"But they need calm and order and routine—"

"Sometimes, yes. But they also need warmth and excitement and the smell of great food in the air around them. I talked to them about this and so I know."

"When did you do that?"

"I dropped by Tom's house yesterday before I signed the papers. I needed to know that they approved with my plans."

Her head was spinning. "And when were you planning to find out if I approved?"

"Now." Robert took her hands. "Please tell me I haven't made the biggest mistake of my life. We can do this, Margo. If you'll only give us a chance."

"You mean give the bistro a chance?"

"Not just the bistro. Us."

"But...I can't believe it. This is too much. Why are you doing all this for me?"

"Because I miss your soup of the day. Because I miss your kids. But mostly…because I love you."

She looked into his eyes and thought, *It's too soon. We haven't known each other long enough to be in love.*

But suddenly she noticed that for the first time in weeks, maybe even months, she didn't have that aching feeling in her stomach. Her head felt crystal clear, too.

Robert pulled her close enough so he could whisper in her ear. "Quit your job, Margo. You don't belong in an office tower. You belong here. And you belong with me."

Was he right? Margo looked around the room. She had chosen everything in this place, from the Garland stove to the last coffee cup. She'd selected paint colors and designed the menu and created all the recipes.

It had been hers, she'd given it up, and now Robert was offering it back to her.

But none of that mattered as much as the other gift he was offering.

Did she dare accept it? Was it possible she could juggle a career she loved, motherhood and being in love, too?

Robert's eyes told her yes.

So did her heart.

*The Singles With Kids group is
meeting again next month!
Look for Nora's story, THE SISTER SWITCH
(SR#1404)
by Pamela Ford in March 2007,
wherever Harlequin books are sold.
Turn the page for a sneak peek....*

"THE SOLUTION IS OBVIOUS," Suzanne said. "You just have to be me."

Nora knew she was in trouble the moment she heard her twin sister utter those words. She tightened her grip on the phone and paced across her small kitchen. "Tell me I just misheard you. Tell me this cell phone connection is so bad you didn't really say what I think I heard."

"You have to do this, Nora. You've gotta take my place."

Irritation rolled through Nora. She'd been supporting her sister for two years as Suzanne tried to build a personal shopping business. Now Suzanne wanted her to *be* the personal shopper? Enough was enough. "Your biggest client wants you to do a rush job for her son. The correct answer is—you get off that cruise and come home."

"I'm on the Inside Passage, remember? Alaska? Open water. Icebergs. You don't just *jump off* cruise ships up here." Her voice grew pleading. "Please, Nora. I can't afford to lose this account."

Nora gritted her teeth. "I know you need this job. I know Camille Lamont is a famous author, and is connected enough to launch your business—"

"So then do the job for me. Think about it. If I keep Camille as a client, it could get me out of your hair—not to mention your house." Suzanne paused. "Maybe then you'd have time to date."

"Suzanne!"

"Nora!" Her sister mimicked her annoyed tone.

"How about if I go to the appointment as myself…and explain that you're on a seventeen-day cruise—"

"No! What will his mother think when she learns I sent someone who knows *next to nothing* about personal shopping to meet with her son?" Suzanne groaned. "I can see this account waving goodbye already."

"Then come back to San Francisco and meet with her yourself," Nora said as evenly as possible."

"We're practically in grizzly territory up here. Probably polar bear, too."

Nora snorted. "I doubt the bear populations will be attacking you at the next port of call—or the airport, for that matter."

"Nora." Suzanne's voice dropped low. "When Keegan called off our wedding, I thought I would die. I need this cruise. Even you said it was a good idea. The Lamont account is important to me, but I'm just not up to it yet. I've only been on the ship for one day. What kind of a respite is that?"

Nora dropped into the kitchen chair as she tried to reason everything out. Suzanne had really hit bottom when Keegan dumped her. And though Nora had never been able to understand her sister's devastation over losing that idiot, she had agreed time away might help Suzanne heal.

Still, that didn't mean Nora taking her place was a good idea. "Suzanne, we may look the same but that's where the similarity ends. I'm a physical therapist. You're a personal shopper. You're loose and carefree. I'm…not."

"I'll say."

"What?"

"Sorry. Sorry."

"Anyway, pretending to be you, even for one meeting, is like…expecting apples to be oranges."

"You didn't used to be an apple. You just became one over the years."

"I did not." Indignation rose up inside her.

"Then how come you keep staying in that hospital P.T. job when you hate it? Come on, I know your complaints by heart." Her voice took on a sing-song quality. "Once people have surgery, all you do is make sure they can use a walker, get out of a chair, and then—boom, they're gone. Discharged. You never see the rehab through to the end."

"It's important work," Nora said.

Suzanne just kept talking. "And what about that new sports medicine rehab center the hospital's opening? They have to hire someone—and you haven't even applied yet, have you?"

The truth in her words irritated Nora more than the know-it-all tone in her voice. "Suzanne, when you grow up you discover you can't have everything. You become—"

"Dull. But you don't have to."

Nora slowly counted to ten in her head. "Whatever. You know what I mean. It's a dumb idea. Switching places is something you do when you're seventeen."

"Or something you do when your sister really needs your help. This isn't about Erik Lamont and you know it. It's about keeping his mother happy. If she wants me to do a quick job for her son, I can't *not* do it." She sighed. "Nora—she'll hire someone else."

"Couldn't you just call her and explain that—"

"Nora? You there? You're breaking up."

"Suzanne? Hello? Can you hear me?" She looked up at the ceiling in frustration. The connection had gone dead.

* * * * *

Happily ever after is just the beginning....

Turn the page for a sneak preview of
A HEARTBEAT AWAY
by
Eleanor Jones.

Harlequin Everlasting—Every great love
has a story to tell. ™
A brand-new series from Harlequin Books

Special? A prickle ran down my neck and my heart started to beat in my ears. Was today really special?

"Tuck in," he ordered.

I turned my attention to the feast that he had spread out on the ground. Thick, home-cooked-ham sandwiches, sausage rolls fresh from the oven and a huge variety of mouthwatering scones and pastries. Hunger pangs took over and I closed my eyes and bit into soft homemade bread.

When we were finally finished, I lay back against the bluebells with a groan, clutching my stomach.

Daniel laughed. "Your eyes are bigger than your stomach," he told me.

I leaned across to deliver a punch to his arm, but he rolled away, and when my fist met fresh air, I collapsed in a fit of giggles before relaxing on my back and staring up into the flawless blue sky. We lay like that for quite a while, Daniel and I, side by side in companionable silence, until he stretched out his hand in an arc that encompassed the whole area.

"Don't you think that this is the most beautiful place in the entire world?"

His voice held a passion that echoed my own feelings, and I rose onto my elbow and picked a buttercup to hide the emotion that clogged my throat.

"Roll over onto your back," I urged, prodding him with my forefinger. He obliged with a broad grin, and I reached across to place the yellow flower beneath his chin.

"Now, let us see if you like butter."

When a yellow light shone on the tanned skin below his jaw, I laughed.

"There…you do."

For an instant our eyes met, and I had the strangest sense that I was drowning in those honey-brown depths. The scent of bluebells engulfed me. A roaring filled my ears, and then, unexpectedly, in one smooth movement Daniel rolled me onto my back and plucked a buttercup of his own.

"And do *you* like butter, Lucy McTavish?" he

asked. When he placed the flower against my skin, time stood still.

His long lean body was suspended over mine, pinning me against the grass. Daniel...dear, comfortable, familiar Daniel was suddenly bringing out in me the strangest sensations.

"Do you, Lucy McTavish?" he asked again, his voice low and vibrant.

My eyes flickered toward his, the whisper of a sigh escaped my lips and although a strange lethargy had crept into my limbs, I somehow felt as if all my nerve endings were on fire. He felt it, too—I could see it in his warm brown eyes. And when he lowered his face to mine, it seemed to me the most natural thing in the world.

None of the kisses I had ever experienced could have even begun to prepare me for the feel of Daniel's lips on mine. My entire body floated on a tide of ecstasy that shut out everything but his soft, warm mouth, and I knew that this was what I had been waiting for the whole of my life.

"Oh, Lucy." He pulled away to look into my eyes. "Why haven't we done this before?"

Holding his gaze, I gently touched his cheek, then I curled my fingers through the short thick hair at the base of his skull, overwhelmed by the longing to drown again in the sensations that flooded our bodies. And when his long tanned fingers crept across my tingling skin, I knew I could deny him nothing.

* * * * *

Be sure to look for
A HEARTBEAT AWAY,
available February 27, 2007.
And look, too, for
THE DEPTH OF LOVE
by Margot Early,
the story of a couple who must learn
that love comes in many guises—and in the end
it's the only thing that counts.

HARLEQUIN® *Romance*®

From reader-favorite

MARGARET WAY

Cattle Rancher, Convenient Wife

On sale March 2007.

"Margaret Way delivers…
vividly written, dramatic stories."
—*Romantic Times BOOKreviews*

———————

*For more wonderful wedding stories,
watch for Patricia Thayer's new miniseries
starting in April 2007.*

Rocky Mountain
BRIDES

This February...

Catch NASCAR Superstar **Carl Edwards** *in*
SPEED DATING!

Kendall assesses risk for a living—
so she's the last person you'd
expect to see on the arm of a
race-car driver who thrives on the
unpredictable. But when a bizarre
turn of events—and NASCAR
hotshot Dylan Hargreave—inspire
her to trade in her ever-so-structured
existence for "life in the fast lane"
she starts to feel she might be
on to something!

Collect all 4 debut novels in the Harlequin NASCAR series.

SPEED DATING
by *USA TODAY* bestselling author
Nancy Warren

THUNDERSTRUCK
by Roxanne St. Claire

HEARTS UNDER CAUTION
by Gina Wilkins

DANGER ZONE
by Debra Webb

**On sale
February
2007**

www.eHarlequin.com   NASCARFEB

Hearts racing
Blood pumping
Pulses accelerating

Falling in love can be a blur...especially at

180 mph!

So if you crave the thrill of the chase—on and off the track—you'll love

SPEED DATING
by Nancy Warren!

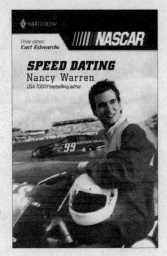

Hearts racing
Blood pumping
Pulses accelerating

Falling in love can be
a blur...especially at
180 mph!

So if you crave the thrill
of the chase—on and off
the track—you'll love

SPEED DATING
by **Nancy Warren!**